STARFELL

Willow Moss and
the Forgotten Tale

Books by Dominique Valente

STARFELL: WILLOW MOSS AND THE LOST DAY

STARFELL: WILLOW MOSS AND THE FORGOTTEN TALE

STARFELL

Willow Moss and the Forgotten Tale

DOMINIQUE VALENTE

ILLUSTRATED BY SARAH WARBURTON

HarperCollins *Children's Books*

First published in Great Britain by
HarperCollins *Children's Books* in 2020
HarperCollins *Children's Books* is a division of HarperCollins*Publishers* Ltd,
HarperCollins Publishers
1 London Bridge Street
London SE1 9GF

The HarperCollins website address is
www.harpercollins.co.uk
2

HARDBACK ISBN 978–0–00–830843–8
TRADE PAPERBACK ISBN 978–0–00–837714–4
PAPERBACK ISBN 978–0–00–830844–5

Dominique Valente and Sarah Warburton assert the moral rights to be
identified as the author and illustrator of the work respectively.

A CIP catalogue record for this title is available from the British Library.

Printed and bound in England by CPI Group (UK) Ltd, Croydon CR0 4YY

MIX
Paper from
responsible sources
FSC www.fsc.org
FSC™ C007454

This book is produced from independently certified FSC™ paper
to ensure responsible forest management.

For more information visit: www.harpercollins.co.uk/green

For dearest Harriet and Julia, who leave
fairy dust wherever they go

STARFELL

MISTS OF
MITLAIRE

LAKE of
the
UNDEAD

SHADOW FALLS

NETHERFELL

1

Leaf-mail

Dear Willow,

By the time you read this, I will be gone. My experiments with cross-pollinating a memory flower with samples from the Great Wisperia Tree have worked. I am happy to report that I can now see ten minutes into the future. Unfortunately, I have just seen that my kidnappers will be arriving IMMINENTLY! Which means, alas, I can't even have a decent cup of tea before I send this letter via leaf-mail.

I once had a rope swing that might have offered a means of escape, but the baby dragon,

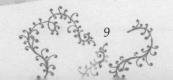

Floss, accidentally burnt it to a crisp during a rather unfortunate coughing fit on his last visit. So I fear my captors are likely to catch up with me soon. (Well, in seven minutes and thirty-three seconds to be precise.)

My attempts at getting hold of the cloud dragons through pepper-tree communication haven't gone according to plan . . . So I thought I'd drop you a note to ask if you wouldn't mind terribly trying to rescue me? Also, could you please look in on Harold while I'm held hostage? He gets a bit lonely when I'm not here. Though he is very capable of feeding himself.

Hope you are well otherwise? The apple-pie blossoms are in bloom again and they always remind me of you . . .

Must dash—
Your friend,
Nolin Sometimes

Oh dear, thought Willow, putting the leaf-scroll down on the cluttered attic table, her heart starting to thud.

The post had arrived in a rather unusual way. Willow had answered a knock on the attic window only to find herself confronted by a rather grumpy oak tree with a face carved deep within its trunk. The tree had scowled at her with thick, bushy twigs for eyebrows, hard knots for eyes and a grim slash of a stick for a mouth. It had made an annoyed and windy huffing sound as it handed over the leafy scroll. Then, after giving her one last thunderous glare that seemed to scorch her very soul, it had slumped back to its usual spot by the garden wall, leaving a steady stream of acorns in its wake – and a fair bit of swearing too. Mostly about being rudely awoken from a rather enjoyable *two-hundred-year nap* and NOT being a blooming *postal service*.

Willow hadn't known that trees could move, never mind *swear* or *deliver mail*. But she'd had a good guess, before she'd even read the leaf-letter, that it had something to do with the forgotten teller, Nolin Sometimes, and the way his rare ability helped him make use of the hidden magic of plants. Still, even Willow Moss, who was used to a bit of odd in her life, had to admit that this was all something of a *shock*.

Willow wasn't the only one surprised by the strange visit. So was her best friend, Oswin, who greatly resembled a cat, but was in fact a kobold – a type of monster – who usually lived under her bed. At this moment, his panicked wailings could be heard from the fat blue stove in the corner, where he had shot off to hide when Willow answered the knock on the window.

'Oh **NO!** Oh, me 'orrid **aunt Osbertrude, WOT** fresh *eel* is this?' (Kobolds regularly overheard popular sayings from beneath beds or other hiding places, but often got them a bit confused.)

Ignoring Oswin, which was sometimes the best approach for general peace of mind, Willow took a deep breath and tried to summon Sometimes from the clutches of his kidnappers. If only he'd said who they were! She concentrated hard, her eyes scrunched up tight, silently begging her magic to work. Though begging hadn't had much effect lately to be honest.

Alas, her face formed a rather regrettable expression that made Oswin snigger behind a fluffy green paw. 'Looks **like yew** needs **the privy.**'

Willow ignored this. Her heart pounded, but, despite how much she tried, her hands remained empty. She just couldn't seem to find her friend . . .

Which was unfortunate, as Willow had a magical ability for finding lost things. Like shoes, or socks, or,

most recently, a lost day that had been stolen by the Brothers of Wol, using a thousand-year-old spell. With the help of her friends, including Nolin Sometimes himself and Moreg Vaine, the most powerful witch in Starfell, Willow had got it back.

But she had never tried to find a missing *person* before. The closest she had ever got to that was when she 'found' Oswin. She had summoned him from a neighbour's stove a few years ago and never quite got rid of him since.

Willow sighed, then glanced at Oswin with a frown. 'Never mind how I look. Nolin Sometimes has been captured!'

Oswin sat up fast, releasing a puff of blue coal dust into the air. In his outrage, his fur went from the colour of lime cordial to bright pumpkin in an instant – one of the side effects of his koboldish heritage. He blinked large, lamp-like eyes and his ears flattened to his skull in shock. **'WOT? Why'd they take 'im?'**

Willow shook her head. 'I don't know! Maybe he's made someone a bit cross or something?'

The kobold shrugged a shaggy shoulder, as the idea of Nolin Sometimes making someone a bit cross was entirely possible.

14

He couldn't exactly help it. As a forgotten teller (or an oublier, to use their official name), Sometimes had visions of other people's memories when he was around them – even the shameful ones. To make matters worse, he then blurted these secrets out loud. He didn't know what was happening when the memories washed over him, so he couldn't control this. Still, it made some people a bit angry . . . *Murderous* even, if the stories of what had happened to some of the other forgotten tellers over the years were true . . . And the trouble was, when Willow stopped to think about it, Nolin Sometimes could have been taken by just about anyone really.

She looked at the leaf-scroll again, as if hoping it would offer something – *anything* – else to help her find him. But aside from a tiny splodge that looked a bit like a flower, where the ink had run next to the forgotten teller's name, there was nothing. Willow sighed and paced the dusty attic floor, leaving a small trail of sock prints behind. Then she tried to use her magic again, hoping that this time it would just *work*. But the problem was that lately it just *wouldn't*.

Unbidden, her sister Camille's voice flared in her

mind. 'Well, *I've* never been unable to use *my* magic before, not even when I had rumble fever and was nearly on my deathbed. But then I suppose it's hard to lose a really *powerful ability*. Maybe yours was so weak, Willow, that all it took to make it disappear was a really good sneeze.'

Willow took a deep breath and pushed her sister's annoying voice out of her mind. She was fairly sure magical abilities didn't just disappear with sneezes.

Mostly sure.

'Just focus, Willow,' she said aloud, picturing her friend's wild white hair, skinny frame, and the way he always had so many pockets filled with strange plants. She tried with all her might to find him, but nothing happened.

Until . . . *something* did.

Something a bit unfortunate, which began with a rather loud popping sound and the familiar wailings of a certain kobold.

'Oh *noooo!'* cried Oswin. **'Oh, me GREEDY aunt, why'd yew CURSE me to live with witches?'** He dived out of the stove and shot into the much-repaired and patched-together green, hairy carpetbag near Willow's feet, which started to shake violently.

Willow shut her eyes, afraid to look. She heard about it, though, soon enough.

There was another loud pop, followed by a bellow from her mother downstairs.

'**WILLOW MOSS**! WHAT DID I SAY ABOUT TRYING TO USE **YOUR MAGIC** BEFORE YOU'VE RECOVERED?'

Willow swallowed. 'Um. That I shouldn't?' she mumbled, reluctantly opening an eye, only to blanch. Most of the attic had vanished. What remained was the single floorboard on which they stood.

It had all disappeared.

From the kitchen below, her mother and oldest sister, Juniper, were staring up at her with identical FURIOUS expressions.

'I – um . . . erm . . . Sorry, Mum,' stammered Willow.

This was bad enough, but things were about to get a whole lot worse rather quickly.

Juniper frowned, then looked at the empty seat next to her and paled. 'W-where's Camille?'

Willow scrunched up an eye, afraid to witness what would no doubt come next. Her mother looked from the empty seat back to Willow accusingly, her lips stretching into a thin, angry line. 'You had better not have made your sister disappear. *Again.*'

Willow bit her lip, then shared a look of commiseration with Oswin, whose eyes were peeking out of the bag in fright.

'Oh *no...*'

2

Magic Most Peculiar

It had started with the spoons.

No one could say for certain if the dessertspoons went first or the serving spoons, but, by the time the teaspoons had vanished throughout the village (and no one could make a decent cup of tea, which was enough reason for anyone to start sharpening their pitchfork), the whispers began to twist their way towards the youngest witch in the Moss family.

In an ordinary village, missing spoons wouldn't cause that much concern, but in Grinfog, home to a family full of witches, it was natural that a few questions were raised. Some with raised voices to match.

Though, as Willow's ability was to *find things*, not make them disappear, she along with the rest of the family had dismissed their neighbours' concerns.

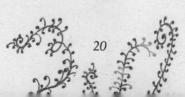

A hiccough in the greening moon perhaps? A band of spoon-stealing poltergeists maybe? Nothing to do with her, though. Until the bunfire on Elth Night, that is, when even Willow began to wonder if she was, in fact, the person responsible for all the weird disappearances.

Elths, not to be confused with elves, are tiny, hairy, bearded creatures – and rather excellent bakers – who live underground. Many years ago, at the precise moment an evil wizard named Wollace Humperdink was passing over their mound, one of the elths' ovens exploded and burnt him to a crisp. Now, all across Starfell, people celebrate the anniversary of this wondrous accident with elthish mushroom mead, 'bunfires' and beards.

Willow had just put aside the gumbo apple and currant bun she'd been toasting and removed her fake, sparkly beard to help a rather persistent neighbour who'd lost her anorak. The woman hadn't quite got the memo that this was supposed to be Willow's *night off*.

Nevertheless, Willow closed her eyes, lifted her palms to the sky and coughed, while she searched with her mind for Birdy Pondwater's misplaced possession.

There was a faint popping sound, but nothing

appeared in Willow's outstretched hands, which was rather puzzling. Willow's magic might not be exciting, but it was always reliable, which was something she'd always taken a bit of quiet pride in. As Granny Flossy used to say, '*A bit of quiet pride does a body no harm. It's the loud pride that can bend a nose right out of joint.*'

Granny Flossy had been full of these sorts of observations. Along with lots of dodgy potions resulting from a cauldron explosion in the mountains of Nach.

Willow pushed up her mental sleeves, eyes still closed, and tried again. 'Don't worry,' she reassured Birdy, who had begun to make a low panting sound a bit like a snuffling wild boar. 'Sometimes lost things just need a bit of encouragement to be found . . . They can get too comfortable there, but I can coax them back.'

Except Birdy would not calm down. She began to shriek blue murder.

Willow saw why when she opened her eyes and found to her utter shock that Birdy's dress had *vanished*, and she was standing in a vest and a pair of rather old-fashioned red-and-white bloomers while the entire village gawped at her, their currant buns left to burn on the bunfire.

'What happened to your dress?' Willow whispered, wishing she had something besides a sparkly beard to offer the poor woman to protect her modesty.

Birdy spluttered, turning violently red, while Willow looked around to see if the wind had blown the dress away. But there was no trace of it. When she turned back, what she saw caused her some dismay, as everyone was staring at her in sudden fear.

Which was a bit . . . *odd*.

While occasionally there was some grumbling about her family's magic, the Mosses were mostly accepted as part of the community – like, say, the way your mother will remind you that your weird aunt with nineteen cats and a collection of dish towels with their faces on them is still, technically, part of the family . . .

A week later, Birdy Pondwater's lost dress landed in Willow's kitchen in a red-and-white flash. She left the dress at Birdy's house, and a kind of stilted peace ensued, in which Willow was far less busy, and far poorer as a result, as most of her regular customers kept well away.

Camille had made the mistake of teasing her about this, which had led to her first disappearance and caused utter MAYHEM until she'd reappeared a minute later with a loud, angry pop.

Willow had never seen Camille so furious. She had threatened to transport Willow to the Mists of Mitlaire – the strange and ethereal fog that separated the world of the living from Netherfell, from which no one returned . . . mostly on account of losing their *souls*. It was a serious threat and Willow had retaliated that if Camille tried that, she'd figure out a way to make her disappear *for good*. At this point, their mother, Raine, had decided to take matters in hand.

'I am taking matters in hand,' she'd said, her mouth forming a grim line as Camille set a feather duster on Willow. It hadn't done much aside from making her sneeze . . . but this had caused Camille to disappear again for a moment, and their mother had decided that the *safest* course of action was to separate them for a while.

'For the time being, I think you can sleep in the spare bed in the attic, Willow. We will get to the bottom of this. You had a cold, and I think that's the most likely culprit – look what happened when you sneezed, and you were coughing at the bunfire . . .' Then Raine had narrowed her green eyes and said reproachfully, 'Though you should not have used your magic if you were feeling unwell. You know this. The number-one rule for any witch who's feeling unwell is what?'

Willow had opened her mouth to protest that she didn't feel unwell, but changed her mind when her mother crossed her arms expectantly. Willow had sighed and recited in dull tones, 'Not to use her magic.'

'Correct.'

As far as witches went, this was a rather good rule, as being under the weather could cause a lot of magical misfires. Willow's cousin, Petulant Moss, who had a talent for rather nasty hexes, had ignored it to her peril when she got a bad case of stutter pox. She had accidentally turned *herself* into a pig, instead of hexing her neighbour – to his delight. It was rumoured that she was still living up north somewhere with rather fluffy, spotted ears . . .

'So, *no magic*, Willow. Understood? Not until we get you better,' Raine had said.

Willow had agreed, and had moved into the attic that morning. She'd lasted half a day.

It wasn't *technically* her fault that she'd broken her promise so quickly . . . As far as she was concerned, the letter from Nolin Sometimes and her fears for him had surpassed her concerns about her magic. In the stakes of wonky magic versus missing friend, missing friend had won out. Or it *should have* if her dodgy magic hadn't made the attic – and her sister – disappear in the process . . .

Luckily, they both reappeared a few moments later. The *lecture*, however, went on for considerably longer.

Willow now sat at the kitchen table while her mother paced up and down, shaking her head and muttering things like, 'I just don't know what's to be done with you. I sent your father word that he should come home so that we can all deal with this together as a family. What if your sister had gone missing permanently? You don't know how to control this – and, despite the risks to all of us, you're *still* using your magic . . .'

'But Mum,' Willow interrupted, feeling a pang of

guilt that her mother had asked her father to leave work early to 'deal' with her, 'I had to use my magic! I've got to find Nolin Sometimes.' She tried once again to explain. 'He's my friend, and he needs me. He sent me a letter—'

'Which has conveniently vanished,' said her mother. She made a '*pfft*' noise, eyes narrowed.

This was true unfortunately. A few things from the attic hadn't reappeared, like Granny Flossy's old purple hat, several tonics that her mother had been forcing her to drink, and the leaf-letter, so no one would believe a word Willow said.

Her mother shook her head and pinched the bridge of her nose in frustration. 'I'd like to believe you, Willow, truly . . . but trees do not *move* or *speak*! I don't know what on Great Starfell made you think they could. Besides that – which is worrying enough – I'm not sure where you got this idea that you've met a forgotten teller . . .'

'Mum, I *have*!' she protested.

'No, you haven't, Willow! It's not something one does. Oubliers are extremely rare, and most end up . . . well, dead because of their abilities, which land them in trouble.'

Willow blinked. '*I KNOW that!* That's why he needs me – it's urgent!'

Willow's mother shook her head, her eyes wide with concern. 'Oh, Willow, I think you're really quite ill. It might be a fever or something that's been causing all this trouble with your magic – and now these *delusions* . . .'

But Willow wasn't ill. She felt fine. She'd had all kinds of colds before and it had never caused her magic to act strangely. Her rogue magic came from something else . . . she knew it. In the back of her mind, Granny Flossy's voice on a cold winter's night whispered, '*Folk that venture into the forest of Wisperia don' always come back the same. I've heard stories of people who changed. Their hair turned to flame, their feet to hooves, their fingers to leaves . . . Forest-touched, they call it . . . They end up having to make a life there, away from everyone they know, as they've turned wild.*'

Willow swallowed. She'd *been* to Wisperia when she'd tried to get back the stolen day. The forest must have done something to her. She tried to push the thought that her hair might turn to flame or her feet to hooves out of her mind, with difficulty.

The problem was getting anyone in her family to consider these risks because, when the lost Tuesday had been restored, so had the usual timeline. No one *remembered* when the day went missing at all, and they didn't know what Willow had done or where she'd been . . . The only people who remembered were those, like her, who had been in the presence of the spell that had brought back the day.

'Please, Mum, just listen to me – I think I know what's happened. I'm going to tell you all about it, and afterwards you'll see what needs to be done.'

She asked them not to interrupt so that she could get through the whole story. To her surprise, they agreed. Mostly, she would find out later, because they'd been trying to gather just how far her fevered delusions went and how urgently they should send for help.

'So you see,' she said, when she finally finished explaining all that had happened a few weeks before, 'I

believe that something affected my magic in Wisperia. It scrambled it around or something. I think, under the circumstances, that the best thing to do is to send for Moreg. She'll know what to do, and how to help me find Nolin Sometimes.'

There was a long pause while her family stared at her in what Willow thought might be amazement at the fact she'd helped to save the world and kept quiet about it for so long, or perhaps even a little quiet pride at her courage in the face of such adversity . . . But it soon turned out to be something else entirely.

Her oldest sister, Juniper, came forward, an odd look on her face as if a beloved pet had died. She felt Willow's forehead and frowned. 'It's the stress, isn't it?' she said, looking at her mother, her mouth in a sad line. 'Ever since Granny passed. She can't face reality any more.' Then for a second her serious demeanour slipped and she clamped a hand to her mouth. 'Oh, I'm sorry . . . I shouldn't laugh as it's really quite awful, but . . . "*send for Moreg*"!'

This made Camille giggle, then whisper loudly, 'She only used her *first name* too, like they were friends! Can you even imagine?'

Willow closed her eyes in frustration. When she

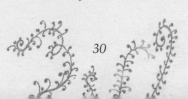

opened them, she saw that her mother's face was serious and rather sad, and she began to explain things as if Willow were still quite little, or possibly *a bit dim*.

'My dear,' she said, patting Willow's hand gently, 'I don't think Moreg *Vaine*, the, um . . . most powerful witch in Starfell, would concern herself with the problems of a twelve-year-old girl.'

This elicited a few more sniggers from Camille and Juniper, but Raine turned and gave her other daughters *A WARNING LOOK*, and they stopped giggling immediately.

'Sorry, Mum,' said Juniper.

Raine's face was twisted with worry. 'What really concerns me is this delusion of yours, Willow. The idea that somehow you and Moreg went off on some wild and impressive adventure together when Granny passed away. I'm so sorry to have to tell you this, but that just *didn't happen.*'

'**WOT?**' blurted Oswin from beneath the table, where he was hiding by Willow's feet, his fur turning a violent shade of orange. '**I** wos **THERE!** She took me **WIFF** 'er in a **BAG** made o' *HAIR*! 'Tis **NOT** made up and 'tis **NOT** about the ol'

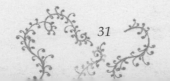

Flossy Mistress, yew ... yew ... CARBUNCLED
CUMBERWORLDS!'

There was a long silence at this.

Then Willow said, 'Thanks, Oswin.' She and the
kobold shared a conciliatory look. Mostly about how
little his outburst would actually help. Still, it was
nice to have someone on her side for once.

Willow's mother pursed her lips in distaste, but
gave no other sign that she'd heard Oswin. This was
her standard approach to him.

It wasn't, however, for Camille. 'Look, just because
you've convinced your *monster* doesn't mean it
actually *happened*,' she snorted dismissively. 'He's
usually hiding away in a bag or under your bed. You
could tell him almost anything had happened and
he'd probably believe you.'

Oswin shot out from under the table to glare at her.
'WOT? Such **LIES!** Such undeservedable **SLEWS**
against me fine **koboldish** character! A curse
upon yeh ... yeh *harpy-hag* – a **CURSE!'**

'Control your monster!' snapped Camille. 'Or I'll
send him away!'

Willow felt her temper go from simmer to boil, and
she stood up fast. 'You will **NOT** touch him. It **IS**

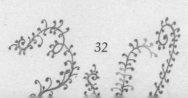

NOT A DELUSION and I haven't *LOST TOUCH WITH REALITY*. Oswin WAS there!'

She took a deep, calming breath, which didn't work, and tried again to get them to see reason. 'It really *happened*, you just don't remember it – but that's only because you weren't THERE! *Because you didn't want to help then EITHER!*'

Camille gave a derisive snort, flinging her midnight hair back. 'Oh really, Willow . . . like we'd not help save the world!'

Juniper made a huffing, dismissive sound too.

Willow sighed. 'Well, you *didn't* because you wouldn't believe me then either. But that's not the point. The way you're all reacting now doesn't make *sense* because you've *seen* what happened. You SAW Moreg – she came here after Granny's funeral. You saw her speak to me and bring me my broom, Whisper, which I only got because I was helping her! How else would I have it? And, before she came, you saw the DRAGONS, so you must know that I'm telling the truth. How else would I have known her, or met a cloud dragon? How else would you explain that?'

There was a long moment when no one spoke.

Then, over the sound of Willow's thundering heart, her mother let out a deep sigh. '*Oh, Willow.* You probably don't know this, but Moreg was a family friend. I grew up with her sister, Molsa, you see. Moreg thought very highly of Granny Flossy. As you know, your grandmother was once the best potion-maker in all of Starfell, which is why Moreg came to pay her respects to all of us when she passed. I believe that she brought you your broom as a gift, to take your mind off Granny's death. I mean, granted, Moreg is not generally known for, erm, spontaneous acts of kindness . . . but that's what it was – a kind act to a child at a difficult time. I'm afraid that, with all the shock and upset, you've got a bit muddled and turned it into something else . . . some wild *story* about saving the world with her, as well as an imaginary friend needing your help, and trees that move and deliver letters . . . Oh, Wol.'

She gave a short, humourless laugh. 'Which is DEEPLY worrying for all of us, don't you see? Because not only do you seem troubled, it's dangerous to be around you as it's affected your magic in a rather violent way. We *have* to get you help, and soon!'

Willow stared at her mother through eyes that were misted by sudden angry tears. There was a lump in her throat, making it hard to speak. She'd never needed Granny Flossy more than she did in that moment. Granny would have made them see, made them hear, *somehow*. She would probably have known the truth about the trees – she knew things like that, things no one else did – and she would have gone outside to try talking to the oak, even if they all thought that was bonkers. She would have trusted Willow, or at least tried to. But Granny Flossy was gone, and there was nothing Willow could do.

Her chin started to shake, and in a very small, choked voice she tried one last time to make them see that she was telling the truth. 'B-b-but you heard what Feathering the dragon said, Mum. About how I helped him. Please can you just –' she sniffed – '*try to believe me?*'

Raine spoke to her in a soft, kind voice, which only made things worse. 'I do believe that, of course I do – the big dragon said that you helped him find his egg. I mean, I think that's a WONDERFUL thing to have done.'

She shot Juniper and Camille a look and they

35

both quickly nodded too. 'We all do,' continued her mother. 'But, you see, it might have been the very excitement of meeting him and Moreg, mixed in with your grief, that caused things to get scrambled somehow . . . and made you think that you'd met before.'

Willow's mouth closed over a wordless scream, hot tears leaking from her eyes unchecked.

They just *wouldn't* believe her. Willow felt her hurt begin to grow as she considered the hard truth about her family. It wasn't just that they didn't believe her: they didn't believe *in* her . . . and they never would. They couldn't even imagine that it was possible for Willow to have done something even slightly remarkable, even with *help*. They would never see her as one of *them*.

She felt winded, as if something hard and jagged had hit her in the chest. The blood rushed to her ears, and there was a ringing sound – later she would wonder if it was the sound of her own heart breaking – and suddenly there was a loud pop.

She looked up to see that she had made everyone, except Oswin, *vanish*.

Meanwhile, somewhere far away, a throne glinted like opals and diamonds in the shadows. Though, if you were to look closer, it seemed to be made of feathers and roots and darkness.

The queen who sat upon it had shadowy eyes like a night devoid of stars. She steepled her fingers and asked her servant, 'You know what you need to do?'

The servant nodded, once. His gaze flicked towards the white-haired man on the floor whose eyes were pale and unseeing, though from his mumbling lips came a low moan.

The queen shifted in her seat like moving ink, and her hair floated in the air above as if she were underwater. She made a motion with her fingers and a small, shadow-like bird flew towards the figure on the ground, and into his open mouth. No more sound escaped his lips.

The servant watched in silence, then turned to leave.

'Be careful,' the queen warned. 'Remember who you are up against. The witch sees all — you must play your game well if you are to succeed.'

'I know what is at stake,' said the servant.

The queen said nothing. She simply lifted a finger. It was the colour of birch bark, silver and dry and stronger than steel. A mist appeared, and there was a flash of wings, and then nothing at all.

3

An Unlikely Accomplice

In the silence between the thunderclaps of Willow's own heartbeats, Oswin stared up at her in horror. **'Oh NOOOOO! Oh, me 'orrid aunt! They'll never believes yew now that yer magic has gon' proper squifflesticks,'** he groaned, covering his large, lamp-like eyes with his paws as if he really didn't want to watch what happened next.

'You're right,' said Willow in a small, scared voice. She swallowed, and took a wary step back from where the table had been, knocking a chair over in her fright. 'Oswin, I'm going to have to find Moreg myself. I think I should go now, quickly, before my father gets here or they come back. I just don't think they'll believe me . . . and, to be honest, right now they're right about one thing. I-I'm a danger to be around. Y-you can stay if you want.'

The kobold went from green to orange in a flash, his eyes shooting daggers at her. '**WOT?** Yew wants to **leave me behind?**'

'No – but you might be safer here.'

Oswin shot her a dark look and harrumphed. '**Wiffout yew 'ere,** that *harpy-hag* will **gets rid** of me **faster** than I could **blink. I'll** take me chances **wiff yew** any day – 'sides,' he said in a small voice, 'yew mights needs me.'

Willow gave him a small, grateful smile. It was true, Oswin could be useful . . . when he wanted to be. Mostly because he was often the one who remembered about food, but there was also the fact that his koboldish blood let him know whenever they were approaching dangerous magic. And yes, there was his rather useful ability to *blow up* when he was agitated enough – which had partly helped save the missing day. Not that he'd meant to do it. Still, it was handy.

Together they quickly packed the hairy carpetbag and left the cottage. Willow stopped only to get her broom, Whisper, from the shed.

At the garden gate, the oak tree harrumphed as she passed him. 'Running away, are we?'

There was a faint **'Oh noooo, *I forgot about 'IM*,'** from within the bag.

Willow turned to look at the tree in surprise, her face blotchy with tears. She'd been sure that he wouldn't speak to her again. She swallowed past the lump in her throat. 'Yes. I need to find my friend, and to do that I have to sort out my magic . . . and get away from here. I'm sorry about the letter, though – and for disturbing you.'

The tree made a windy harrumphing sound. Then its knot eyes softened slightly as it took in the state of Willow's tear-streaked face. 'It sounded like you'd been punished enough.'

'You heard all that?' she asked, surprised.

'Trees hear everything,' he replied, then raised a root from the ground. 'I reach well under the cottage . . . I know what's going on, even when I sleep.'

Willow didn't know what to feel about that. This whole time they'd had an audience they had never known about. It was a bit creepy when she thought about it.

'I know it really happened – the missing day,' said the tree. 'If that helps. I know you aren't talking nonsense . . . well, no more than the rest of them

41

anyway,' he said, pointing a branch in the direction of the cottage. 'I felt that something was wrong, that something had disappeared, causing strange effects, even as I slept. And, besides that, trees talk . . . We know what you helped to do.'

Willow blinked. *They did?*

There was a loud popping sound from the direction of the cottage, followed by several high-pitched screams. Willow's heart started to race – her family must have reappeared in the kitchen. At least this still allowed her a bit of a head start. Fighting mounting panic, she picked up the carpetbag with Oswin inside. 'I'd better go – I can't afford to waste time hoping that my family will believe me. My friend needs me.'

The old oak tree considered her. 'I was the youngest in my family before I moved here . . . An oak needs some space sometimes,' he said, pointing to the dark woods ahead. 'I remember how it was – no room to grow. I'll hold them off while you leave.'

'You will?'

He nodded, making his leaves rustle. 'Didn't much care for that comment about trees to be honest. As if it was ridiculous somehow. Typical of humans to think only they can talk or move or think . . .'

There was a harrumph of agreement from within the carpetbag at this. **'*Exacterly,*'** mumbled Oswin.

As the tree frowned at the bag in some confusion, Willow stared at him. 'But how will you hold them off?'

There was a windy sort of grunt. 'I'll think of something,' he said, shuffling some acorns in a slightly menacing way that made Willow feel a moment of concern for her family, and even guiltier than she already did for running away.

Still, he was giving her the chance she needed.

'Thank you,' said Willow.

The tree ignored her thanks as it clomped towards the cottage, muttering to himself, 'Blooming had to choose a house full of witches, didn't I? Couldn't just keep my darn roots out of it . . .'

Then, as the cottage door opened, despite his grumbling, the oak began pelting her family with acorns rather enthusiastically while they all screeched in shock. Seeing Willow, they shouted at her to come back.

'Willow, don't go!' cried her mother, dodging an acorn. 'Stop, you horrid tree!' she snapped as another one bounced off her forehead. 'Willow, I'll get Amora Spell to come and look at you – we can do something about this! I believe you about the tree at least . . .'

But Willow shook her head. It was too late. Besides, Amora Spell, her grandmother's swindling ex-partner, would definitely not help matters and time was running out. She needed to get to Moreg. It was possible that the witch knew where poor Nolin Sometimes was.

As Camille stepped forward, the tree picked her up and said, 'Oh no you don't, missus . . . I have half a

44

mind to drag you off to the Mists of Mitlaire myself for threatening your sister with that. A person's soul is no joking matter!'

Willow swallowed down her guilt. 'I'm sorry, really . . . but I have to go!'

Then she mounted Whisper and set off towards Moreg's house, her family's screeches and Oswin's loud, panicked cries of '*Oh noooooooooo, **not this flying sticks** again!*' heavy in her ears.

Far away, in a strange place where time seemed to have stopped, Nolin Sometimes woke to darkness. It was the kind of dark where you can't see your own hand in front of your face, where you aren't sure where you begin and the shadows end, or if they end at all . . .

He swallowed as he sat up. There was a lump throbbing on his forehead.

The silence around him was unlike any he had ever known or grown used to in the forest of Wisperia, where there was always the sound of birds, the rustling of trees, the whisper of the wind . . . This was the absence of all that. It was nothing.

He called out to the nothing . . . which was when the fear started to build to a crescendo and the blood rushed in his ears, for no sound escaped his lips, even as he screamed . . .

4

Pimpernell, a 'Hed' Witch

As Willow flew up, past the dark woods and towards the warm glow of the midday sun peeking behind the trees, the hard knot twisting her stomach seemed to loosen slightly.

While she regretted having to leave her family behind in such a dramatic way, she felt a sense of purpose grab hold of her. It was the first time she'd felt anything like it since she'd found out about what had happened on that missing Tuesday – when she'd discovered that she'd lost Granny Flossy and the world had seemed to end.

Up through the trees, the wind in her hair, everything seemed to grow quiet, allowing her mind to sharpen, and she began to think.

And the main thing she thought was that she should have brought a *map*.

47

Willow reached into her pocket and took out her StoryPass, a magical device that resembled a compass and appeared to know things that she didn't. It seemed to agree, as it was currently pointing to *'One Might Have Suspected as Such'*.

'Do you think I should head east or west for Troll Country?' she asked aloud. A green paw shot out of the bag, palm up, followed by a mumble about not exactly

being able to *see* properly through a bag made of hair.

Also something about a cumberworld.

'I suppose we'll have to land and ask for directions,' said Willow, pointing Whisper down towards a village on the edge of the woods.

But, as she began to descend, a flock of ravens helicoptered from the sky, making bloodcurdling cries that made her stomach take a dive. With a horrid

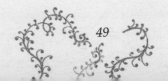

thrill, Willow realised they were aiming straight for her, as if she were some rather large prey they'd quite like to gobble up.

'What ON WOL?' She screamed and twisted the broom till she veered away from the village below and almost flew straight into a clump of trees, earning herself several scrapes and scratches as she collided with a branch. She righted Whisper and tried to go back towards the village, but the ravens continued to circle her, making their odd cries.

In the hairy green carpetbag, she could hear high-pitched wails from Oswin. 'Oh **NOOOOO! Oh,** me 'orrid aunt, I don' **wanna die** as **bird food!**'

Heart pounding, Willow flew in the opposite direction through low branches, twigs smacking her in the face, until they crash-landed with a thud in a thick pile of leaves. Willow tumbled off Whisper, and the broomstick came to a halt a few feet away.

From her landing place, she looked up in immense relief to see the ravens soaring away, the air full of their eerie cries. With a shaking hand, she shaded a palm against her forehead, and noticed that one of the birds had a strange wing that appeared blue and made of something like smoke. She blinked, and it was gone.

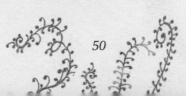

Still breathing rather heavily, she dusted herself off, wincing as her grazed palms stung. Then she picked up the hairy green bag, which harrumphed. **'WOT** was that **abouts?'**

'I don't know,' whispered Willow, who was having a hard time convincing her legs that they should move. She'd never known birds to behave that way. 'I think it might be safer if we go by foot for a while.' She fetched her broom, which was covered in mud and leaves, and put it over her shoulder with a frown.

It was late afternoon when she neared a clearing in the woods. She could see a hand-painted sign that read:

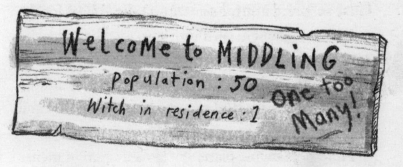

'Hmmm, it doesn't seem like these are the type of villagers who'd appreciate another witch on their doorstep,' said Willow, looking at the pink graffiti that had been added by some daring soul to the bit about a witch in residence.

Oswin agreed. 'Let's **SKEDADDLE!**'

Willow turned to go back the way she'd come – only it was too late. There was a loud clanking sound from behind her that caused the hairs on the back of her neck to stand on end.

'Wot do we have here? Another witch, yeh say?' hissed a voice that made her knees forget for a moment how to hold up her legs.

Willow turned, stumbled and swallowed. In that order. Her eyes widened, and stayed that way. She could well understand how *this* could be one witch *too many*. *More than enough.* She was like every rumour that you might have heard when it came to the word 'witch', every idea that set your skin to gooseflesh, every nightmare, all rolled into one. Though there wasn't a wart on her chin or a tall black hat on her head, somehow, from deep within Willow's chilled

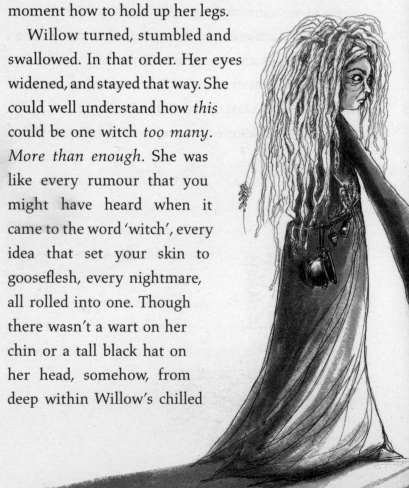

heart, she felt that the figure before her had all the allotted witchiness that could have been reserved for, say, a rash of witches. Or a botherment. Or, yes, a coven, if one wished to use the proper collective noun.

She was very tall, with long silver dreadlocks that fell down to her waist. She had skin the colour of dried almonds, and strange amber eyes, like wood snapping in a fire, which blazed into Willow's, pinning her to the spot. There was a strange clanking sound when she walked, which was somehow unexplained by her long copper-and-silver-coloured robe, and she moved with the aid of a large opal-topped cane.

'*Ohnooonooooo*, *a curse upon yeh*, **Osbertrude!** *This is jes* **NOT** *turnin' outs ter be a* **good day** *to be a* **kobold,**' cried Oswin, who zipped himself more securely into the carpetbag and began to shake in fear. Invoking the curse of his aunt always meant serious danger was coming.

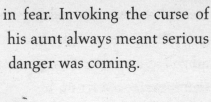

The witch's wood-fire eyes seemed to glow, and she spoke slowly, in a spooky yet lyrical voice that caused gooseflesh to rise all over Willow's body. 'Wot yeh doin' down here in these woods, child?'

Willow tried to explain, while also attempting to mentally persuade her knees to stop knocking. 'I-I need to get to Troll Country. I-I was going to look for a map, or ask for directions.'

The witch narrowed her eyes. 'Troll Country, yeh say, hmmm? That be MIGHTY interestin'. And just wot do yeh want with Moreg Vaine, child?'

Willow blinked. 'H-how did you know that?' There were not many people who knew that the most fearsome witch in all of Starfell chose to live in a secret castle within a valley in Troll Country ...

'Pimpernell always knows, child . . . and wot she don' know she finds out soon enough.'

Willow frowned, and the witch explained. 'That's me name. Blu-Scarly Pimpernell, ter be precise, though most call me by the latter. I'm a hedge witch round these parts.'

'*Oh noooooo!* A hed witch?' muttered Oswin from the bag, which begin to shake even more. 'A brain scrambler? Let's SKEDADDLE!'

The witch rolled her amber eyes at the bag. 'A hedge witch, kobold. Not *head*. I'm a healer – use things that grow in these here hedges ter make people better in me healing tower in the woods, don' yeh know.'

Willow's mouth fell open in surprise.

The witch turned to give the village a dark look. 'Them there don' quite know wot they been missin' all this time, as I got a knack fer colds and such-like. I don' just fix magical people's maladies . . . well, not by choice anyway.'

Willow frowned. *Pimpernell* . . . She'd heard that name before, hadn't she? Hadn't Granny said something about her? She racked her brain but nothing came to mind.

Pimpernell looked at Willow and said, 'So tell me 'bout it, child. Wot's been eatin' yeh?'

Willow bit her lip, wondering if she could trust the witch, and decided *perhaps not.*

'Um. Nothing. I'm absolutely, completely fine. I just need to find Moreg. I need her help with . . . something.'

The witch's strange, fiery eyes raked over her. 'Fine, yeh say?' She shook her head. 'I don' buy it, child. Yeh don' look well, if yeh don' mind me sayin'

so – peaky-like. Somethin' wrong with yer magic if yeh asks me . . .'

Willow blinked. 'H-how did you know that?' she gasped.

'Pimpernell can always tell. 'Sides, I can help yeh with that, child – no need ter bother the witch . . . She's away, last I heard, so yeh'd be wasting a journey anyway. 'Sides, I been missin' me spectacles for ages, so yeh can repay me by findin' them once I've helped yeh. Is that a deal?'

Willow nodded. That sounded fair.

It was only much later, when it was too late, that she realised she'd never told the witch what her power was . . .

5

The Wizard Beyond the Wall

At first, as Willow followed the witch into the heart of the Howling Woods, she thought that maybe visiting a healing tower before she tried saving Nolin Sometimes wasn't the worst idea in the world . . .

Though there was a tiny part of her that looked at the tall, fearsome witch and her imposing tower, which was covered in moons and stars and *gold glitter*, and thought . . . was all this really necessary? Wasn't it just the sort of thing that made people without a magical ability a bit suspicious of those who had one?

Still, it wasn't exactly an opinion she dared venture out loud.

'Come on in, child,' said the witch, leading Willow into a bright and airy room on the first floor of the tower. It was filled with rows of steel beds and sleeping patients who were quietly snoring.

Willow's eye fell on the witch's foot as she walked in front, her steps making that *clink-clank-clink* sound as she moved. Willow caught a glimpse of something that seemed to glint, like metal.

Pimpernell saw her looking and twitched her dress back over her foot. 'This way,' she said, and the witch made Willow sit on a low stool while she took down a large bottle of tonic from a heaving cabinet full of all sorts of dried herbs, potions and cures.

On a long wooden table nearby there was a pestle and mortar and several odd things in jars. Some of them gave Willow the creeps, like one that seemed to be full of eyeballs that were regarding her rather intently. Willow swallowed nervously. From the hairy green bag there was a faint **'Oh no.'**

The witch handed her a steaming goblet, which smelt a bit like feet. 'This be one of me best blends – sorts out most problems pronto-like.'

Willow took a sip and shuddered rather violently – which was when things went wrong rather *fast*.

As soon as the tonic touched her tongue, the bottle and spoon vanished with a loud pop. The witch looked at her suspiciously, and suddenly more and more

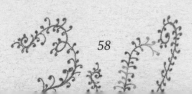

items in the tower began to disappear. The witch started to wail in fear as beds, mugs, carpets and plates all began to vanish.

'Wot yeh doin', child! Stop it!' she cried, but Willow couldn't. The table went. Then the cabinet. People started to wake up, falling to the floor and screaming as the beds beneath them disappeared. It was pandemonium in seconds.

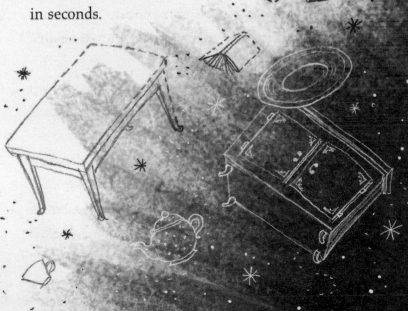

The witch blinked at her, then seemed to nod. ''Tis a bad case yeh got here . . . Extreme measures will need ter be taken! But I'm gonna help. We'll get this tempest outta yeh, one way or another, child! I'll have ter get yeh outta here pronto, though. Ter the top with yeh – there's nothin' much up there so it won' matter if yeh make it disappear.'

With that, Pimpernell picked Willow up as if she weighed nothing and whisked her up the stairs, making a *clinkclankclinkclankclink* sound as she ran. The witch shoved Willow and her hairy carpetbag into a room at the very top of the tower and quickly locked the door.

''Tis fer yer own good, child!'

'Oh no! **Oh NOOOOO,** oh, me **'orrid** aunt!' cried Oswin, from where the bag had landed on the cold wooden floor.

'*Oh nooooooooooooooo,*' was pretty much how Willow summed up their current predicament as well.

As the heavy attic door was bolted behind her, Willow was just working up to a full, panic-heavy scream of her own when a smoky, gravelly sort of voice interrupted.

'*Psst, girl.*'

Willow turned round in surprise, but couldn't make out where the voice was coming from. She squinted into the gloom.

'*Over here,*' said the voice.

Willow looked. But all she saw in the small room were dusty wooden floorboards, on top of which sat a small iron bed with peeling green paint, a chair, a small table stacked with old newspapers and, in the corner, an old green stove covered in cobwebs. Propped up next to this was a poker shrouded in dust.

There was no one there.

Her glance flicked upward, towards the rafters, where there were some rather large spiderwebs. She swallowed nervously. 'Um?' she whispered.

'On yer left,' said the voice.

The hairy carpetbag began to shake. **'Oh noooooooooo, me greedy aunt! Wot new eel is this?'**

Willow's breath caught in her throat. What new eel indeed? Had she somehow been locked up inside a dangerous witch's tower *with a ghost*?

'Lass, yer other left, here,' said the voice, sounding slightly exasperated.

To the slight relief of her knocking knees, she saw a gnarly finger waving at her from a small hole in the

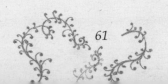

wall opposite. At least it wasn't a *ghost*, though the lone finger wasn't exactly comforting either.

Willow hesitated, then came forward slowly. Kneeling down on the attic floor and putting her hair behind one ear, she peered through the hole. She could just make out a sea-green eye and, when the figure turned, a heavily lined and weathered face framed by long, straggly grey hair. She felt her heart rate return almost to normal. It was just an old man. A wizard, she realised, if he was *here*.

'Whatcha in for?' he said, his blue-green eye wide.

'Oh. Well, you see, my magic has gone a bit weird—'

The sea-green eye narrowed. 'How weird?'

'Um. Very? It's sort of scrambled, I think. Usually, I find things that are lost, but lately . . . well, erm, it's almost as if I'm making them vanish as well.'

The face turned and she saw the wizard head-on. He was even older than she'd first thought, with one eye made of glass, but his expression was curious, and his other eye was clear and full of life. 'Well, are ya?'

'Yes. I – I suppose I am,' said Willow, who, even now, after everything that had happened, was finding it hard to admit that *she* had been the cause of the missing things. 'But *NOT* on purpose.'

'Ah, that's the problem, see. If it were on purpose, ya wouldn't be stuck up here,' the wizard said with a humourless snort.

Willow couldn't deny the logic of that. 'Pimpernell said she'd help . . .' This now seemed a bit doubtful. 'When I met her in the woods, I thought she seemed, well . . .'

'Helpful?' supplied the old wizard with a hollow sort of laugh, as if he knew an unwelcome secret she did not.

'Yes.' Willow frowned as she recounted the tale to the wizard. 'She made it seem like she could help me, but I think she started panicking when I made half of her tower disappear.'

To be fair, Willow thought, panicking did make a bit of sense . . .

'The witch means well,' acknowledged the wizard. 'The problem is that she can take trying to help to extremes. Especially if she thinks you're dangerous.'

Willow swallowed. Locking someone up did seem extreme, especially considering the only reason things started to disappear was because Pimpernell kept trying to force Willow to drink that dreadful-smelling tonic.

Suddenly she remembered what Granny Flossy had said, and what her brain had been trying to remember. *'She's one of the best healers around, but 'tis hard living on yer own. Especially when you don' feel accepted by the people around you – a body needs company, and outsiders, to make 'em see wrong from right. It's not good to only take yer own counsel, and Pimpernell has only been listening to herself fer years . . .'*

Willow stared at the eye in the hole. 'Do you think she'll let me out?'

'Oh. I dunno,' said the old man, rubbing his chin

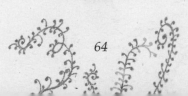

in thought. 'Hard to say for sure, but once she's figured you're a danger it'll be hard to persuade her differently.'

'Oh,' said Willow, her heart sinking fast.

'Me name's Holloway, by the way.'

'Willow.'

'Who's that with ya?' Holloway asked. 'Thought I heard someone else.'

'That's Oswin. He's a kobold,' said Willow, pointing to the hairy green bag behind her.

'A kobold!' he gasped, his sea-green eye brightening. 'Well now, ya don't see that every day.' There was silence and Holloway admitted, 'Not that I can see him now, as he seems to be in a bag, but ya know what I mean.'

There was a low mumble from Oswin about **'peoples forgetting that *not* seeing kobolds is the whole points of being the monster from under the bed'** – or monster in the bag as he was more recently known – and then something about cumberworlds.

Willow shrugged at Holloway's confused look. She was too distracted by the thought of *getting out* to explain.

She got up and tried the door.

Holloway sighed. 'I've wrecked two chairs and a table trying to break open my door, but nothing works. I think they've been charmed shut. And unfortunately—'

'You can't undo a charm from the inside,' said Willow, sitting down in despair. She'd learnt that the hard way too.

'Yup.'

She took the StoryPass out of her pocket and wasn't surprised to see that the needle was currently pointing to '*One Might Have Suspected as Such*'.

'Well, that's just perfect,' she sighed.

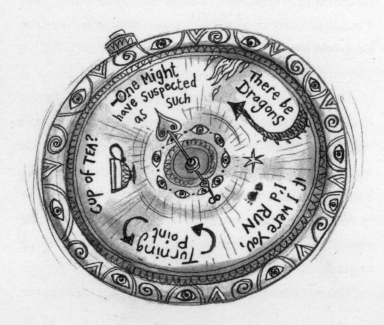

Still, that didn't stop Willow trying to break out. By the end of her first day, she'd used the poker to try prising open the lock on the door and had broken the chair against it too. She'd even attempted scaling the walls of the tower – several times – but to no avail.

'Like I said,' continued Holloway, as if no time had passed, when she collapsed in a heap with her head in her hands, 'she's taken every precaution necessary so we can't get out. See, there's four levels to this tower. This is the last, for the highly dangerous and incurable. Each level goes in ascending order. First is yer everyday sort of maladies, like spell-rash or love-potion recovery. Second is stubborn curses. Third is environmental—'

'Environmental? That doesn't sound so bad,' said Willow.

'*Pfft*,' scoffed the wizard. 'That's one of the worst! Ya know – those poor souls who spent too much time in the forest of Wisperia, where magic went to hide after the Long War? They come back with leaves for fingers, stalks for eyes, or worse . . .'

Willow felt her heart thud. Did they also come

back with their magic turned *inside out*?

'Then again,' Holloway continued in a dark whisper, not noticing her distress, 'they're not half as bad as the ones who wandered through the Mists of Mitlaire. They haven't really come back, have they? Just their bodies.'

Willow shuddered. She'd heard the stories, of course, about the poor souls who were lost to the Mists, the ghostly veil between worlds where time seemed to stand still. Families who were never able to find their loved ones again. It was said that beyond the Mists was the Lake of the Undead, which flowed into the shadowy realm of lost souls, Netherfell.

It was the stuff of nightmares.

Willow cleared her throat nervously, and tried to push the thought out of her brain. 'How come you're in here, Holloway, and, erm, in the most dangerous section?' she asked, darting a wary glance at Oswin, whose green head had peeked out of the bag. He made a motion with his paw for her to get away from the wall, fast, which she managed to ignore. *Just.*

'I was trawling for fleurie-coral with me boat when I had a run-in with a sea serpent, and I lost me leg, again.'

Willow blinked. 'Did you say you lost your leg, um . . . *again?*'

'Yeah, well, me wooden leg – was a good one too. Fitted perfectly, not like this blasted one, which pinches something terrible. Lost me real leg years ago when the Great Melee Sea froze and I got exposed to the bitter cold. Life of a sailor,' he said with a woeful shrug. 'But this latest escapade was far worse, as not only did I lose me good wooden leg, I developed this weird thing where everything I touched turned to copper.'

'*Copper?*'

'Yeh. I know, right? Gold would have been worth the fight. Anyway, I came here when I heard about Pimpernell. Heard that she might be able to help put things right, and, for a while, that seemed true. She found these dragon-scale gloves that helped – stopped me changing things – which was great. It got me thinking that maybe I didn't actually need a cure for me new ability – I could make use of it. Trade with it, that sort of thing. So I told her thanks and said I wanted to be on me way. But she got sticky about it. Told me that she couldn't let me leave if I was going to be a danger to others. I told her that with the gloves

I wouldn't be harming anyone . . . Well, she didn't see it that way. She got suspicious, thought I was up to no good. Like maybe I would use me new ability against people. There was a confrontation, and she tried to get the gloves back from me so that I would stay. I resisted, of course – but she got them off. I tried not to touch anything, but, I mean, that's hard, ya know? I stumbled into a few beds, which turned everything – the sheets, the floor and even her *foot* – to copper.'

Willow gasped. So *that* was what had happened to the witch's foot!

Holloway sighed. 'She used a potion throw on me – ya know the kind ya don't even need to drink for them to take effect? Something for sleep, I think, as I passed out. Next thing I knew I woke up here.' He gave a short, humourless laugh. 'She'd put the gloves back on me, but she took her foot as proof that I was a danger and needed to be kept here for me own good. She told me that it was for the best while she works on that cure . . . which I'm beginning to think might never happen. It's been about a year now.'

Willow gasped. *A year? Here?* 'I'm so sorry, Holloway! It was an accident. She must know that – you never meant to do it and, if you've got the gloves, then surely you aren't dangerous? Can't you explain that to her?'

'Yeh . . . well, I tried, didn't I? She didn't see it that way. She didn't trust me any more. And, I suppose, because I'd tried to get the gloves back and flee, perhaps she had reason not to,' he said in a hollow voice.

'Still, that didn't give her the right to keep you here,' said Willow.

He nodded. 'The trouble is this whole tower has been charmed to do her bidding, so it's impossible to go against her and –' he sighed, sounding hopeless – 'truth be told, I do feel a bit like I deserve it. I feel really bad about her foot.'

There was a heavy silence after this. Willow could only imagine. 'But it wasn't really your fault,' she said again.

Perhaps Holloway had needed to hear that because after a while there was a sniffing sound, and he mumbled, 'Thanks.' Then he cleared his throat. 'Maybe you'll have better luck – she's true to her word, even if she's a bit extreme. If she thinks you're no longer dangerous, she will let you go.'

Willow shared a fearful look with Oswin. If the

witch had locked up the wizard for a year for turning things to copper, how long would she be stuck here for making things disappear? And, while she was imprisoned here, what was happening to poor Sometimes? They were wasting time! He'd trusted Willow to rescue him, and who knew what danger he was in? Moreg's dark words, when she'd told her why so few forgotten tellers were around, floated into Willow's mind. *'Most don't live to tell their tales . . .'*

She put her head in her hands. She had to get out. She had to find her friend before it was too late.

Nolin Sometimes woke once more to silence. His eyes turned from unseeing white to blue, and he saw shapes in the darkness.

It was his forest, his home . . . only it wasn't. The trees and plants seemed made of shadow and smoke. He sat up in what might have been his garden except

that it was devoid of all colour, and he frowned. There was the sleeping Sharon, only he couldn't hear her gentle snores, and her palm-like fronds remained oddly still. There was the memory flower he'd used recently, restored yet lifeless. It looked . . . wrong somehow.

It was all so quiet – so horribly quiet. He swallowed. How long had he been here? Days? Weeks? Months?

He felt so alone. He thought of his friends and bit his lip. He hadn't had many friends, not for years. He'd convinced himself it was safer that way, but the truth was not many people wanted a friend like him – someone who could tell all their secrets. Yet somehow, not long ago, a young witch had come into his life and all that had changed. He'd met people who liked him as he was, and didn't seem to mind that he was a bit different.

He felt his throat close with tears . . . He didn't want to be here any more. He just wanted to go home, tend to his garden and plants, and give his dog, Harold, a hug.

'Please,' he tried to whisper, to whoever was keeping him here. 'I won't bother you, or tell your secrets, I promise. I only hear people's memories

when I'm near them – I don't go out of my way to share what I learn with anyone later. I'm not like that. Please, just let me go . . .'

'Oh, that's not something you need to worry about. I'm happy for you to share all that you know,' said a strange, echoing voice. And this was when the world began to spin, and a figure stood before him – a beautiful, otherworldly creature, her hair blowing in an imperceptible wind, thistles sprouting near her feet. She crouched down and touched his wild white hair. If she had an expression, it might almost have been kind.

Except, as she continued to hold her hand against his head, he realised that she wasn't there to look after him, but to take something instead. Suddenly his memories grew loud, and the roots that wound round him seemed somehow to carry his secrets to her. He tried to resist, to thrash, but it was impossible.

'Don't try to fight it,' she said, almost kindly, a birch-bark-like finger touching his temple.

He tried to protest and his eyes turned white again, though no sound escaped his lips.

6

The Tower Fights Back

Over the next two days, Willow was forced to swallow tonic after tonic, and sample all manner of vile, evil-tasting 'cures'. None of which made any difference. Things still randomly seemed to disappear – like her coat and her nightdress, which was rather annoying as all her efforts to get them back failed too.

Food arrived through a little chute in the wall.

'It minimises escape attempts, ya see – the tower helps her do it,' Holloway had explained, peering at her through his hole in the wall.

It didn't stop Willow trying, though. When the witch wasn't bringing tonics and ignoring her pleas to release them, Willow was putting all her efforts into trying to break out. So far there had been thirty-two failed attempts. The last one had involved getting Oswin to blow up the door, with no success.

This had resulted in a somewhat frosty exchange between them for most of the day, as the only way to get Oswin to blow up was to insult him enough. Mostly this involved *crossing the line.*

Which is exactly what Oswin said, drawing a dusty line with a sharp rust-coloured claw on the floorboards. **'This is the line,'** he hissed, his fur pumpkin-bright, smoke curling off his ears and his huge, lamp-like eyes full of fury. Then he drew a little cross above it and said, **'AND THIS is when you calls me *A CAT.*'**

'Sorry, Oswin,' she said. *Again.*

'How's it going with you, Holloway?' Willow asked, changing the subject.

The wizard had decided if he couldn't break out of the tower, he'd at least try and break into her room so they could all be together.

'I'm making progress,' he said, and she saw that there was now a much larger hole in the wall, twice as big as the wizard's straggly grey head. He winked. 'Won't be long now!'

She grinned back.

Early the next morning, there was a small yellow flash and Willow's coat appeared in a heap on the floor. She picked it up, surprised to find that it was muddy, and smelt of dirt and flowers. She frowned. Where had it been this whole time? And, more importantly, how had it appeared without her even thinking of it?

She was distracted from her thoughts by a *clink-clank-clink* sound, followed by a *screech* as the attic door was unbolted and the witch bent her silver dreadlocked head to enter the room.

As quick as she could, Willow shoved the broken chair and the bag with Oswin inside it in front of Holloway's now *rather large* hole in the wall.

The witch looked at her suspiciously as she jumped back. 'Come stand here, child, where I can see yeh.'

Willow did as instructed, and the witch unstoppered the cork of a new tonic. The rich scent of cabbage and something sour, like rotten fruit, filled the air.

'Smells like boiled socks . . . and the privy after yer father's been at it,' whispered Oswin.

Willow wrinkled her nose.

'I want yeh to drink this, and no complainin' this time,' said the witch, narrowing her eyes. When Willow hesitated, Pimpernell sighed. 'Always makin' it hard, aren't yeh? I'm only tryin' ter help.'

'Help?' cried Willow. 'How is this help? The only one making this hard is you, keeping me *prisoner* here for no reason!'

The witch's wood-fire eyes looked sad yet resigned. 'Child, I had ter do it or yeh would have made the whole place go! Yeh need my help, and I'm gonna give it ter yeh whether yeh likes it or no. 'Tis for yer own good. 'Tis not like I'm enjoying this. Truth be told, I thought we'd have found somethin' ter sort out yer magic by now, but 'tis a stubborn case . . . just like you are, child. But don' yeh worry – Pimpernell always has a plan up her sleeve.' Then she clicked her fingers and the iron bed marched forward and trapped Willow against the wall.

There was a faint **'Oh no,'** from the hairy green bag.

Willow could barely breathe as the iron headboard pinned her arms to her sides. *'Aaargh, let me go! None of this is working anyway! I've tried all of those disgusting tonics, and nothing's happened!'*

The witch shuffled towards her, her silver cane and copper foot going *clink-clank-clink* as she neared. 'It will work if yeh give it a chance! We just gotta be patient. We'll find the right one and yeh can be cured, if yeh just open wide.' And she advanced with the tonic, ready to pour it down Willow's gullet if she had to.

Willow shook her head frantically as the vile-tasting tonic began to froth. The witch clamped a strong hand on her jaw and began to dribble it on to Willow's tongue. Willow closed her eyes, thrashing wildly as her senses filled with the stench of rotten fruit, her heart thundering in her chest – and then, suddenly, there was a loud popping sound.

'Oh n— OH!' breathed Oswin, peeking out from the bag at the noise, turning from pumpkin orange to a bright lime green in relief, though his ears were still faintly orange. **'Oh! Yeh *did* it!'**

Willow opened her eyes, then blinked in bewilderment as she saw that the witch and the bed that had been pinning her . . . had *disappeared*.

'**Come on, let's SKEDADDLE!**' suggested Oswin.

The tower, however, did not want to let them go. Not without a fight. It sent a bedpan and a chair flying at her and Oswin, who turned a violent shade of orange in his outrage.

'*Aaargggggh!*' Willow screeched as the iron poker leapt from the floor and hurtled towards her, pricking her in her side. 'Ouch. Stop it! Stop this right now!' The poker slowed down, but continued to poke her wherever it could find a gap. She batted it away with her arm, earning herself countless scratches in the process, as it kept prodding her into giving the tower back its witch. Only . . . *she couldn't*. She wasn't sure *how*.

Oswin wasn't having the best time either. He was fighting off several rolled-up copies of the *Middling Times*, which were repeatedly smacking him over the head. His ears were starting to smoke in a rather worrisome way, which usually meant he was on the verge of blowing up. '**Oi,**' he said as one of them thwacked him on his ear. '**Stop that!**'

Thwack.

'**A curse** upon yeh!'

Thwack.

'**A curse!**' he growled.

Thwack. Thwack.
Thwack.

Finally, Willow
screamed, '*Ouch!*
Eugh. Stop. Just
STOP! Enough
of this, Tower. Or
I will make you
disappear too!'

The rolled-up newspapers above Oswin's head seemed to sag. One of them smacked him rather feebly on the forehead one last time, and he hissed a low warning, his flame-orange fur standing on end. The poker, meanwhile, paused before Willow's feet, the top bent towards her in a hangdog sort of way.

'Um, thank you,' said Willow, rubbing her arm, which was starting to sting from all the scratches. 'Now I suggest you open the door and let us out.'

The door remained stubbornly shut. It juddered on its hinges somewhat reproachfully.

She narrowed her eyes, crossed her arms and, summoning her fiercest voice, declared, 'If you do not OPEN this door right NOW, I will NOT release your witch.'

There was a long pause, while Willow tapped her foot impatiently, and then, with the faintest of clicks and a slow, reluctant creaking sound rather like a sigh, the door opened.

'Good,' said Willow, hiding her relief that it had worked. She helped Holloway climb through the wall, breaking some more of the plaster with a chair leg so that he could get his shoulders and torso through. Once he was clear, she grabbed Oswin by his long tail and shoved him back inside the green hairy carpetbag, to his outrage.

'**Wot** choo go an' **grabs me by the tail** like that **for!**' he harrumphed. '**Wot wiff** being **thwacked on me** 'ead and **monster-**'andled **like** that, there's jes **no** respect, me being **the last kobold** an' all!'

She ignored this, and together she and Holloway dashed out of the room and down the stairs before the tower could change its mind – or the witch popped back from wherever Willow had sent her. Whichever came first.

As soon as they were outside, the thirteen-foot tower door slammed itself shut with a loud BANG, and then bolted itself for good measure. Perhaps it was hoping that she wouldn't change *her* mind and come back either. Then it sort of bent a little, like it was looking down at her rather expectantly, and Willow realised with dread that it was waiting for something . . . something she couldn't exactly deliver. The windows looked on reproachfully.

Willow bit her lip. It was a bit odd that the witch hadn't actually reappeared yet. When she'd made her family vanish, they'd returned in mere minutes. It had been triple that amount of time already. She blinked as she realised something. The truth was she didn't really *want* to find the witch – not just yet. And, now she thought about it, when her family had come back, they'd reappeared *in the house* rather than next to her, like missing things usually did. Could that have been because she'd needed to keep them at a distance in order to escape? She didn't know if her wishes had anything to do with the way this misfiring magic worked or not.

'Um,' she hedged, clearing her throat slightly, 'it might take some time, I'm not sure . . .' She thought of her coat and nightdress, which had taken a couple of days to reappear. 'I'll find her somehow, erm, as soon as I figure out how to actually do that.'

The iron bar that ran along the middle of the door seemed to fold itself together, like someone crossing their arms. Then the door-knocker shaped like a witch's hat turned itself into a mouth and stuck its tongue out at her.

Willow blinked. '*Rude!* It's not like you treated me any better, locking me up like that . . . and anyway I didn't mean to make her disappear. I was provoked, and—' Then, catching sight of Holloway's raised eyebrows and Oswin's wide eye peeping out of the carpetbag, she blushed. She realised that she was trying to justify herself to a *building*. Shaking her head at herself, she said, 'Come on, let's just get out of here.' And they set out towards the Howling Woods, towards freedom, at long last.

It was only later that Willow realised with a heavy heart that she'd left behind her broom, Whisper. But it was too late to go back, and besides she was sure that there was no way the tower would give it back if she didn't give it its witch in return.

7

The Sudsfarer

They walked for close to an hour.

'If we go this way, it'll take us to a small tributary of the Knotweed River, where I keep me boat,' said Holloway.

Willow swallowed. If what Pimpernell said was true, and the witch really did seem to know everything – like Willow's ability, and the fact she had a kobold in her bag – then Moreg was gone, which meant that Willow was going to have to find Nolin Sometimes some other way. It couldn't be helped. She figured the best

place to start looking was where he'd been taken.
Perhaps there was some clue left behind. She might
even be able to find a plant that could help fix her
magic. Now that she thought of it, if any garden
could hold a cure, surely it would be his?

'I need to get to Wisperia,' Willow said.

The old wizard's eye fairly popped out of his
skull as he twisted to look at her. 'Lass, ya don't
want to go there, trust me!'

'I have to, Holloway. My friend needs me –
he's in danger . . .' She swallowed. She hadn't had
that many friends before, and after losing Granny
– Willow felt her stomach clench at the thought
of her, but tried to push the feeling away – she
couldn't, *wouldn't* risk losing anyone else. 'He's
counting on me.'

It meant a lot to her, more than she could say.

The wizard's eye shone in the morning light, and
he nodded. 'I can take ya up the Knotweed, towards
the Cloud Mountains.'

'Thank you,' said Willow.

'No problem. It's the least I can do as payment
for breaking me out. But, if ya come back with
leaves for fingers, don't say I didn't warn ya.'

Willow gave him a slightly strained smile. It was too late for that anyway, wasn't it? She only hoped she wouldn't make her magic worse by going back.

It was past midday when they reached the edge of the thick forest where a river was bordered by reeds and grass. It smelt of salt and marshland.

As they hacked through the bulrushes, they encountered the thick, cloying knotweed that lent the river its name. It was a creeping plant with rather delicate purple flowers shaped like bells.

'Whatever ya do, don't listen to the music,' said Holloway as a tinkly bell chime began to play from the water. 'It'll lure ya under, to the merworld.'

'Merworld?' Willow breathed.

'Yew **don'** wanna go there, **trust** me,' hissed Oswin, his shaggy head popping out of the bag. '**Still got** the scars.'

Willow blinked, looking at the kobold in surprise.

'**Long** story,' he muttered. '**Almost** found meself married, like **I don'** have enough **troubles** being the **last kobold** anyhow. They got teef like nails . . .' He shuddered.

Willow started to grin, not sure what to make of

that, but, when the sound grew louder, she clamped her hands over her ears to block out the knotweed. Shifting the carpetbag to the crook of her arm, she waded deeper into the river until she was standing up to her thighs, her shoes soaked through and her teeth chattering from the cold. Still they kept going, their feet slipping on mud, which left them dirty and tired. At last Holloway led them to something large and bulky that was obscured by a small mountain of foliage, which he started to remove.

'Me boat,' he explained, his sea-green eye gleaming. 'Had to camouflage it, in case someone tried to pinch it.' He cleared the last of the debris, and Willow blinked in shock. It didn't look like a boat.

It looked like an ENORMOUS copper bathtub with silver feet. The bridge, though, appeared to be made from several large, round cauldrons held together somehow by magic to form, quite frankly, the weirdest boat Willow had ever clapped eyes on. The copper glinted and gleamed in the sunlight. Jutting skyward was a copper weathervane topped by a large figure of a whale that had turned a blueish green over time. Willow forgot for a moment that she was bone-cold or covered in mud as she gaped at it.

'It's not traditional,' said
Holloway, clearing his
throat at her silence.
'It's brilliant!' said
Willow.

The tops of the old wizard's cheeks turned rosy with pride. 'Made it meself,' he said, beaming.

Holloway offered her a gloved hand so that she could get aboard, using a set of steps that had been buried in the marshland too. Then he untied what looked like a collection of old handkerchiefs knotted together, with a massive blue-green copper kettle attached to it, which had acted as an anchor, and climbed aboard himself.

As soon as he did so, a wind from nowhere began to stir, and a set of similar yet tiny copper kettles threaded above the helm lit up like a string of fairy lights.

Willow looked around in amazement. The bath-boat reminded her a bit of her brief experience in the Ditchwater district in the city of Beady Hill where home-made houseboats had lined the waterways, though she hadn't seen any quite like *this*.

'Welcome aboard the *Sudsfarer*.'

Faint music began to play from an old harmonica that was sitting on a battered wooden drum. It sounded a little tired as it gave a feeble sort of hoot.

'Got rusted,' said Holloway, picking it up sadly. Then, after pulling off one of his gloves, he touched it.

It immediately turned to bright, shining copper and began to play in a livelier way that made Willow's foot tap in response, despite the fact that she was wet and cold.

'That'll do,' he said to the harmonica, and the instrument fell silent with a slight *duh-dum* for Willow, who grinned widely.

While Willow was still marvelling at this, the wizard laid a hand on the large copper wheel inside the helm and said, 'Up the Knotweed River, *Sudsfarer*, all the way to the Cloud Mountains.' Then he winked, and put his glove back on.

There was a giant lurch and the bath-boat began to scuttle forward like a giant copper hippopotamus as it made its way towards deeper water.

'Oh NOOOO, oh, me greedy aunt!' moaned Oswin, a paw covering his eyes as he turned a sickly shade of green like cabbage soup.

Willow gasped. 'The legs move!' She stood by the lip of the bath-boat and peered down, watching them in fascination as they trundled in the water, and the bath-boat started to swim against the gentle current the deeper it went. Holloway cast a sail made of several patchwork quilts, which gusted to life, and

they began to hurtle up the river at breakneck speed.

Holloway grinned like a proud parent as the wind blew back his straggly hair. 'Traded Rubix Grimoire for the charm that brought it to life – turning it from a simple bathtub-boat into *this*. Wasn't cheap!' he shouted, pointing at his glass eye.

Willow paled, clutching the side of the bath-boat for safety as it hurtled across the water. She knew Rubix Grimoire – she was her mother's friend, and the guardian of Willow's friend Essential Jones. Rubix was a witch who specialised in charms, and took the craft *very* seriously, even living in a strange star-shaped home. 'You gave her your EYE?'

From the carpetbag there was a loud gasp.

Holloway shrugged. 'It wasn't doing me much good. C'mon,' he said, motioning for her to follow him, and Willow saw to her surprise a small wooden door leading to a whole area beneath the deck that she hadn't noticed till then. She turned to follow him, taking a firm hold of the side with one hand and clutching the carpetbag in the other. Oswin was still staring after the wizard from the hole in the bag in horror.

'*That's jes mad,*' he whispered.

94

Willow couldn't help but agree.

She was distracted, though, from the tale of the wizard's eye as she made her way carefully down a set of copper steps to the cabin area and started to feel rather green. 'I might be sick,' she said as the world started to spin.

'Hagsbreath! Apologies,' said Holloway, who gave the side of the boat a tap with his fist. 'Slow it down there, boat, we have *guests*. Easy does it.'

And the boat obliged, decreasing its speed to a smooth, leisurely pace.

'Thanks,' said Willow gratefully, though it took a moment for her stomach to settle. Then she was able to appreciate the downstairs area more.

It was surprisingly spacious. There was a small galley kitchen with gleaming copper pots, pans and kettles. At the back of the kitchen was a window, beneath which was a small wooden table. A little way along the galley was a small sitting area with two armchairs, one blue, one green, with multicoloured patches on the arms. Between these was a small copper card table that was set up with a pack of brightly coloured cards spread across its polished surface, and right at the back of the boat was a separate cabin, with

a curtain for a door, behind which was a small bed.

Holloway took a kettle from a rack above an old fat stove and carried on their conversation from above as if no time had passed. 'It was a clouded eye, the one I gave her. So, to be honest, she did me a favour.'

Willow frowned. 'What do you mean?'

'Couldn't see properly out of it. It turned everything grey and, well, cloudy. Me mood too – like the world became miserable whenever I looked out of it. I used to wear an eyepatch just so that I could see and feel things normally. Luckily, it came out easily – it wasn't like a regular eye. It just popped right out after a bit of fiddling . . . Made this squelching sound, though, that was a bit alarming.'

Willow and Oswin both made horrified faces. To be honest, until then Willow hadn't wondered how he'd got his eye out.

'Anyway,' carried on Holloway, not noticing their dismay, 'now I see all the colours of things, no clouds at all. I'd say that's worth it!' He beamed.

Willow could see how that might be possible. It couldn't have been fun to have every day seem clouded.

'But why did Rubix want it?' she asked. 'Doesn't

seem like the kind of thing a person would have a use for.'

'Beats me,' said Holloway. Then, running a gloved hand through his hair, he shrugged and said, 'But why does a witch do anything?'

'Practical makes perfect,' said Willow, thinking of Moreg and how she always seemed to be a few steps ahead of everyone else.

Holloway gave her a puzzled look. 'What's that?'

Willow shook her head. 'Just something a witch once told me.'

'Nutters, the lot of 'em,' muttered Oswin from within the bag.

The queen looked up as her servant arrived. He looked different, changed somehow. There were dark shadows beneath his eyes, and he was thinner than he had been. The queen noted this with some interest.

The servant held her gaze. 'The witch has arrived. She is with your wraiths . . .'

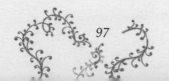

The queen sat back in her throne, satisfied. 'That is good news indeed. You have done well.'

The servant hesitated.

The queen narrowed her eyes. 'What is it?'

'I-I just worry this seems . . .'

'Wrong?' asked the queen.

He nodded. 'Yes.'

'The fate of the world depends upon this. You know that. You knew it when I asked you, and you know the rewards,' she said, waving a hand. A smaller throne appeared by her side.

He frowned and the queen said, 'You will have a place here. A home.'

He nodded. It was what he'd wanted for so long. He turned to leave, adding, 'The girl is on her way.'

The queen looked satisfied at this. 'See that she is.'

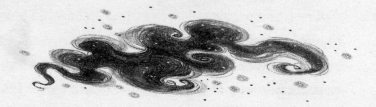

8

Rain Biscuits

Willow had just come back from the end cabin, where she'd changed into dry clothing, when it started to rain, the sound heavy on the copper roof.

Holloway got excited. 'Grab a pot – hurry!'

Willow did as he suggested with a puzzled look on her face. 'What? Why?'

'No time to explain! Quick,' he said, opening up the window in the galley kitchen and leaning far out with a pot to catch the rain. 'C'mon,' he said, and Willow fetched a blanket from the armchair (no point in getting wet again, she reasoned), and put it over her head before she stood on the table and shoved a copper kettle out of the window. It didn't take long for the pots to fill and, when they brought them back inside, the old wizard's lined face was lit up with happiness.

'We'll be able to make rain biscuits with this! Best ship's biscuit around,' he promised.

Willow blinked. *Rain biscuits?* She shot a look at Oswin, who was peering at them from the green armchair where he'd set up camp, a blanket tucked up to his chin. The kobold shook his green head and whispered, **'The gizard's** *lost the* **plot.'**

Willow blinked. It did sound a bit impossible. 'Erm, Holloway, how will we make biscuits with water?'

To her surprise, the wizard began to laugh, slapping a knee in his mirth. 'Not water, lass. Rainwater. And rainwater that has bounced off the Knotweed River – which is particularly delicious, you'll see. The weed might be deadly if it strangles ya, but it tastes great.'

Then he started rooting around in the cupboards, bringing out a big mixing bowl, flour and something that looked like powdered butter. Next, taking a copper spoon, he started to mix everything in with the rainwater they'd collected. 'Well, don't just stand there gawping – make yourself useful. First rule of the sea: no idling.'

And Willow grinned as she helped him to shape the dough into large, spurgle-sized pieces before they popped them on to a baking tray and into the oven. Half an hour later, the fresh scent of rain and something sweet like vanilla perfumed the air.

Twenty minutes after that, Willow placed a piece of warm golden biscuit on her tongue, and her eyes closed in bliss. It tasted sweet, and fresh, like a rainstorm mixed with honeysuckle. 'That's amazing,' she said.

'**Yep,**' said Oswin, who'd been drawn to the kitchen by the promise of food. He stood on the counter to gather up six of the warm biscuits, which he shovelled into his wide mouth, treating them all to a rare, cat-like grin. '**Very tasties.**'

'Old sailor recipe,' said Holloway. 'We've all had to learn to make food virtually from air or water when we're out at sea.'

As the afternoon drew on, Holloway leant back in the green armchair with a smile on his old, worn face, a cup of pepper tea steaming in his hands, and said, 'Nothing tastes as good as freedom.'

'Mebbe **chocolate** cake,' considered Oswin. '**Wiff sprinkles.**'

When they looked at him, he shrugged. '**Wot?** I means ... *almost* as good.'

Holloway snorted, then looked around him with a puzzled look on his face as he picked up his mug. 'Where's the spoon?'

Willow's heart started to thud.

'Ah, here on the floor. Never mind,' he said. Though, seeing her ashen face as he sat back up, he asked, 'What's wrong?'

Willow swallowed. 'I-I thought for a moment that I'd made it disappear.' She explained about what had happened with the spoons in her village, and that it was because of her, though she had no idea how she'd done it.

'Ah,' said Holloway. 'Ya know, I've been thinking about this problem you've been having with yer magic, and I wondered if maybe you've considered that it's something else?'

'What do you mean?' Willow asked.

'Well, ya say that yer ability has always been to find lost things, right?'

'Right.'

'Well, it doesn't make sense. I mean, first of all, ya seem perfectly healthy to me. No cough or sniffle, right?'

She nodded. 'I had a little cough, but that's been gone for weeks. I think it might be because I went to Wisperia.'

'You've been there *before*?' exclaimed the wizard, sitting up in surprise. He looked at her more closely, perhaps to see what sort of a person she really was. As Granny Flossy had said, only those who were mad or desperate went there . . . and she had been desperate

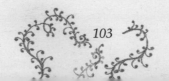

to find the missing Tuesday.

'Yes,' said Willow, and she explained a little about meeting Nolin Sometimes and the dragon, Feathering.

To her surprise, Holloway shook his head. 'I doubt it was that to be honest. People only tend to get magical maladies from Wisperia when they start experimenting with the forest, or spend too long there. A day or two wouldn't do much. I think—' Then he paused and gave a small shake of his head. 'Never mind. Not me place really. Maybe I imagined it.'

'What?' asked Willow. 'You can tell me.'

Holloway pursed his lips. 'Well, for it to play up like that . . . There's only one thing I've ever known that can do that to a person.'

'What's that?'

'Grief.'

Willow felt sudden tears prick her eyes. There was a long moment in which she didn't say anything – *couldn't* say anything. Her eyes filled, and Holloway looked like he wanted to go back in time and erase his words.

He bit his lip. 'I'm sorry, lass. I said it wasn't me place – I'm an old fool at times. You just look really sad sometimes is all.'

Willow shook her head. 'No, you're not a fool, Holloway. I-I . . . I lost my Granny Flossy recently.'

As she said her grandmother's name, it felt as if the air were snatched from her lungs and she forgot how to breathe. It happened like that sometimes, the remembrance of her. Some days it was something as small as seeing a tiny green shoot in the ground that was exactly the colour of Granny's hair that did it. Other times it was the scent of a stewed grumbling Gertrude – the dark purple fruit that the old woman had used to improve the flavour of her dodgier potions – that suddenly brought tears to Willow's eyes. These little things would make her stop suddenly, like her legs were wading through churned butter, and she couldn't move – not until her heart remembered how to beat again.

She wondered if that would ever stop – if she would ever just think of Granny Flossy and not feel as if the world had somehow ended. When she'd found the missing Tuesday and discovered that she'd lost *her*, Willow felt as if she'd lost a piece of herself in the process too.

She swallowed and willed herself not to cry. *Not here. Not now.* She'd been doing that a lot lately. She

gritted her teeth. She had to be strong.

'I'm really sorry to hear that, lass,' said Holloway, his sea-green eye full of remorse. 'It's not me place to say, but I figure that might be what's at the heart of it, and I'm afraid the only cure for that is time.'

Willow bit her lip, trying to encourage the tears to retreat. Perhaps Holloway sensed this as he put on a bright voice and suggested they play a game of cards called Witchstyx.

There were four sets of different cards: a witch's hat, a broom, a cauldron and a raven.

'They're a terrible old stereotype . . . about witches,' he said, his cheeks turning slightly red. 'I mean, I know most witches don't subscribe to the old ways any more.' He cleared his throat.

'**Only** cos **they** can't, w o t wiff what 'appened ter **magic** after the war,' sniffed Oswin from the opposite chair. '**Else this** one woulds 'ave it **all,** 'cept mebbe the hat. That would look a bit weirds.'

Willow shot him a look, but her mouth twitched as she tried not to laugh.

Oswin was right that since the Long War a thousand years ago, when magic was almost completely destroyed, magicians were not as powerful as they'd

used to be. The magic that had returned to Starfell centuries later wasn't like the magic of old, which had gifted people with many abilities. It had learnt not to trust humans, and only gave small traces of itself. This was why most people who were lucky enough to have magic in their veins these days only had the one ability, like Willow.

Oswin was right, though, that she'd always fancied the old traditions, particularly brooms. Though she wasn't sure about ravens – that sounded dead creepy . . .

'All ya have to do is match like with like and shout "Witchstyx" first. It's fun. Ya win regardless, though, if ya get this,' Holloway said, shuffling the pack and showing her a beautifully drawn card of a fearsome witch. '*Umbellifer. Queen of the Undead.*'

Willow took the card and her eyes widened. The ghostly ruler was depicted as a skeletal figure. There were dark holes where her eyes should have been and

on her head was a crown made of bones.

'She's 'orrid,' said Oswin, looking at it and shivering. **'The stories!'**

Willow agreed. They were dreadful. All good ghost stories began with the Queen of the Undead. Still, it didn't stop them trying their best to get her card as they began to play.

Later in the evening, after their fourth round of Witchstyx, Holloway sighed as he sat back in his armchair. He crossed his wooden leg over the other, then grimaced as he fiddled with it.

'Is it hurting you?'

'Some,' he admitted. ''Tis not the same as the one I had made in Lael. Elves, ya know? They know how to make things that work. Fitted me skin like a glove, moved when I moved. This just chafes something rotten. Do ya mind?' He looked at the leg and then at her.

It took Willow a while to realise he was asking her if she would mind if he took the artificial leg off – and she realised that he'd been keeping it on this whole time, despite his discomfort, for her benefit. She felt terrible. 'Oh, Holloway, please take it off – you don't have to wear it for me! Is there anything I can do?'

The wizard sighed in relief as he popped it off and gave the skin beneath it a rub. It looked red and painful. 'Thanks. Not really, though, not unless ya can find me old one! Lost it to that darned sea serpent. Life of a sailor, always doing battle with something – be it sea or *sea monster*.' He gave her a good-natured wink.

Willow bit her lip. He did say that it was *lost*.

Then, before she could even raise her hand to the sky to try and find it, a great cascade of water fell from above and something solid landed with a *thunk* on the floor.

'WHAT IN WOL'S NAME? Is that mine?' exclaimed Holloway, looking down at the wooden leg. It had a few bite marks, possibly from the run-in with the sea monster.

Willow blinked in shock. How had she done that without even thinking?

'Th-thank you,' stammered the wizard as he took up the leg. Then he hopped to the kitchen, dodging the great puddle of water where the leg had landed, and started filling up a kettle with water. 'I'll just give it a quick rinse before I put it on. Who knows where on Starfell it's been!' he said.

He washed the wooden leg tenderly with soap and water, then patted it dry. When he put it on, Willow could see the difference immediately. It fitted like a glove.

He looked at her in amazement. 'I know things aren't going according to plan with yer magic, but I can say this for nothing. Despite what you've told me about yourself, yer magic is far from ordinary, and I'm grateful *as*.'

Willow blushed to the roots of her hair at the compliment. But really, as she got up to fetch a mop to clear up the water, she was just relieved, considering the current state of her magic, that she hadn't somehow made him or the boat disappear instead.

When night-time rolled around, Willow set up a bed on the floor, using the mound of cushions from the armchairs, topped with a large patchwork blanket. Holloway had offered to give her his bunk, but it didn't seem right to take the old wizard's bed.

As Oswin made himself comfortable at the foot of the makeshift bed and Willow plumped up one of the cushions, she couldn't help wondering aloud, 'But how did I make it happen? Finding his wooden leg, I

mean. I didn't even really try, and when I do it doesn't seem to work.'

'Mebbe that wos why it worked. Yew din't try,' said Oswin, rolling over to get more comfortable. 'Yew jes *did* it.'

Willow sat up fast, her heart thudding in her chest. Was the kobold right? She thought about her friend, Nolin Sometimes, and tried *not* to think, while she attempted to summon him from the clutches of his kidnappers.

Then . . .

'Rats!' whined Oswin as the mound of cushions disappeared with a loud pop. Then he scowled at her, his fur turning bright orange. 'DIN'T I JES SAY IT 'APPENS WHEN YEW *DON'* TRYS?'

'Sorry, yes, you did,' said Willow. She was forced to share the blanket with Oswin, who glared at her in annoyance for five minutes straight before he finally turned to go to sleep, muttering something about cumberworlds.

9

A Conspiracy of Ravens

Morning came early on the bath-boat, with the sound of birds flying overhead and river weeds rustling as they cut through the water at a steady speed.

Willow sat at the helm with a cup of pepper tea and watched the sky turn from pink to gold as the world went by, her ears steaming slightly from the hot drink. Her body ached from its uncomfortable night on the copper floor of the boat. Unfortunately, the cushions had only reappeared at dawn.

Holloway stood by the wheel, his face turned towards the sky. 'Can't bottle that – been a long time since I felt the wind on me skin.'

Willow grinned. 'Where will you go now that you've got your freedom?'

'Anywhere me heart takes me. That's the beauty of it.'

She nodded. That was. It made her think of poor Sometimes, captured and taken who knew where. Willow frowned. She just hoped that when she got to Wisperia there would be some clue as to where he was. She looked at her hands and sighed. If only her magic would just *work*.

In the distance, she could hear the strange cries of a raven. She looked up, thinking of the group of birds that had forced her off course and into Pimpernell's path, and saw there were some circling the boat. She breathed easier when they flew on overhead.

Oswin's grumbling stomach told her to think of more earthly pursuits, and she attempted to rustle up something for breakfast. She found a dented, dusty old tin of ven beans right at the back of one of Holloway's mostly empty cupboards.

'Beans for breakfast it is,' she said with a slight grimace.

It was past noon when Holloway took out a copper spyglass and looked not at the horizon, but up above, at the whale weathervane, which was currently pointing to **M**.

'M?' Willow asked, peering at it.

'Magic,' he said. 'It's a useful guide at times. I got it from the town of Library. Fascinating place, not like you'd imagine. It's where they keep all the magical books in Starfell. I reckon if ya wanted to know any of Starfell's secrets, particularly about magic, that's the best place for it.'

Willow's eyes widened. That was where Moreg had got the StoryPass too. It sounded like an interesting place to visit.

She looked up again at the weathervane and her brow furrowed. The ravens were back. They were circling overhead, and she remembered what Moreg had told her once.

'*A group of ravens are often called an "unkindness of ravens", but I prefer the less well-known term, a conspiracy.*'

A conspiracy of ravens had always sounded like *trouble*, and Willow felt the hairs on her neck stand on end.

'It's strange for them to be out here,' Holloway mused, raising his spyglass to have a closer look. But, as soon as he did, the ravens vanished in a flash. Willow blinked. Were they following her? But that was mad . . . wasn't it?

The air filled with mist as afternoon descended, and a single raven emerged from the gloom above, making a strange, almost warning cry. It was followed by several more, and she almost fell over.

'Great Starfell!' cried Holloway.

The ravens seemed to be carrying something. As Willow squinted into the mist, she thought she saw something long and thin, and . . . were those white feathers at the end?

Then, the next thing she knew, whatever the ravens were carrying landed with a soft thump on the deck in front of her. She looked up and saw that they were all departing, apart from one raven with glossy black feathers. One of its wings was strange, almost as if it were smudged, or made of dark blue smoke. It landed on the lip of the bath-boat and let out a hoarse caw, pointing its beak towards the floor.

Willow looked down, then gasped. 'Whisper.'

'Why must we whisper?' hissed Holloway, eyeing the raven, who was staring at them very solemnly.

'It's my broom – it's called Whisper,' she said, picking it up reverently. Then she looked in shock from it to the bird, except, suddenly, there wasn't a bird there at all.

There

was

a

boy.

10

Sprig

They stared at the boy in shock. He was scrawny, with dark eyes and hair. His clothes were old and tattered, yet it was his left arm that drew Willow's eye. It looked like it was made of blue-black river sand, as the skin was pebbled and marked with concentric scores. As she stared, he made to cover it with a shirt that had been tied round his waist and she felt bad for staring.

'You're Willow?' he asked.

His voice was like the raven's cry, low and oddly haunting.

She nodded. 'H-how did you know?'

'Moreg.'

Suddenly Willow remembered something. It was a morning she would never forget, when she'd left her cottage with Moreg to find the lost day. Ravens had circled above them then too, in the dark woods. Among them Willow had seen a strange one with a dark, smoky blue wing . . . and then the witch had raised a finger and seemingly made the bird disappear . . . This was him.

Willow stared as she realised. 'Moreg sent you?'

'Yes. She told me to give you that,' he said, pointing at the broomstick in her hands. 'Said you'd need it.'

Then he turned to leave, and a shudder went through his body, followed by a ripple and a flash. For a moment there was a trace of feathers, then his body shuddered again and he was back to being a boy.

He sighed and sat down by the side of the boat. 'Would you mind if I rested here a while? It's been a long journey.'

Willow shook her head. 'Of course not.'

She looked at Holloway for confirmation, who nodded and said, 'Stay as long as ya need, son.'

Willow went to fetch the boy a glass of water, which he accepted with gratitude, downing it in one. 'Thanks,' he gasped.

What did it mean, Moreg asking this boy to bring her broom, Whisper? Where was the witch? Did she know about Nolin Sometimes? Why hadn't she come herself?

'Do you know where Moreg is?' Willow asked. 'Can you take me to her? I need her help. Our friend has been taken – it's really important.'

The boy looked up at her, his eyes glazed with fatigue. 'She—' His eyelids started to flicker. He was struggling to keep awake.

Holloway said, 'Poor lad looks tuckered out. C'mon, it can keep a little while. I'm sure he'll tell ya everything when he's rested.' And he led the boy below deck to sleep.

The boy slept well into the evening, while Willow paced outside the bedroom, waiting.

'**If the** witch s e n t yew the **broom, mebbe it** means **she's** working on **getting** the forgotten teller **back** too,' said Oswin.

Willow nodded. That was true. She bit her nail, wishing the boy would just wake up so she could ask him if that were true, if the witch had some kind of plan for rescuing Nolin Sometimes.

'C'mon, lass. Nothing to be done right now – might as well have some dinner,' added Holloway.

The boy woke at last to the scent of fish frying in the small kitchen. The wizard had speared a ferntail, which was large enough to feed everyone comfortably.

The boy ran a hand nervously through his dark, messy hair as he found them all sitting just outside the bedroom. Willow had been playing a round of Witchstyx with Oswin, trying to distract herself from her impatience, but when he reappeared she stood up so fast that she made her chair wobble.

The boy didn't notice. He just looked round and said, 'This is some boat.'

'Thanks,' said Holloway.

'I'm Sprig,' said the boy. 'I didn't introduce myself properly earlier, sorry.'

'You were tired,' said Holloway. There were still deep circles beneath the boy's dark eyes.

Barely containing her impatience, Willow tried to be polite. 'This is Oswin, and Holloway,' she said quickly, indicating the old wizard with his long grey hair and glass eye, who waved a spatula at Sprig in greeting.

Sprig smiled. He seemed to find the sight of Oswin the most diverting, and couldn't help staring. The kobold looked up from matching a cauldron card with one of Willow's, his green fur turning ever so slightly orange at the edges, and said, **'Wot?'**

'I've just never seen a ca—' He broke off at Willow and Holloway's violent head-shaking.

Willow mouthed, *'Don't call him a cat!'*

The boy's eyes widened, but he nodded and seemed to hide a grin as he said, 'I just haven't seen that game played in a while is all.'

The kobold nodded, his fur going back to green.

Willow cut to the chase. 'Do you know where Moreg is? I need to speak to her urgently. My friend is missing and I think she might know something about it!'

Sprig's eyes widened. 'Oh. I – um, no . . . She didn't say anything about that to me. Besides, she's gone – some Enchancil business. Be away for a while, I gather.'

Willow felt her heart sink down to her toes. The Enchancil was the official body for magical people in Starfell, short for Enchanted Council.

Sprig added, 'All she told me was that you needed

your broom – that it'd help you. She told me it was in a tower and paid me to bring it to you. I'm sorry – that's all I know.'

Willow's brows knitted in thought as she considered his words. Not many people knew it, but Moreg Vaine, the most powerful witch in Starfell, was a seer. She saw visions of things before they happened. She must have known that Willow would need her broom, perhaps to find Sometimes . . . If the witch wasn't coming, maybe it was because she'd seen Willow finding him? Was that it? She tried to draw courage from this.

'Right. Well, in that case, I think I should head off to Wisperia straight away,' she said, going over to get the carpetbag.

But Holloway came forward and put a hand on her shoulder to stop her. 'It's late now. No point trying to fly in the dark – you'll need a clear head to pass through Wisperia, trust me. Have an early start at first light.'

Willow bit her lip. The old wizard's words made sense, but she still had to fight the impulse to jump on Whisper and fly through the night.

'You're telling me,' said the boy. 'Wisperia is

dangerous enough when you can see where you're going.'

Willow nodded and took her seat opposite Oswin again.

'Anyway, food's ready,' said Holloway.

Sprig sat on the edge of the kobold's armchair and, when Holloway offered him a plate of food, he took it gratefully.

Oswin looked up at the boy suspiciously. Generally, people liked to keep a bit clear of kobolds due to the rather persistent smell of boiled cabbage, but Sprig seemed to ignore this. Perhaps ravens didn't smell that much better.

'Could you always turn into a raven, or did it develop later?' asked Holloway.

'Um, since birth. I'm the only one in my family who can.'

Willow shrugged. 'My ability only came when I was about six.'

Willow had heard that some people – like Nolin Sometimes's family – seemed to pass down their abilities to their children, but it wasn't usual. It only happened with some forms of powerful magic.

'It was random in mine too,' she said. 'We've all

got different abilities, some more powerful than others.' She didn't admit that hers was the least powerful of them all.

'She finds lost things,' added Holloway.

Willow shrugged. 'It's useful.'

'I'd say,' said Holloway, tapping his leg. 'Been missing this for at least two years now, and just like that – *poof* – she made it appear!'

She smiled at Holloway, glad at least that she had made the old wizard happy.

For a long time she'd wondered if there was only so much magic to go around, so that by the time her mother had had her last child only the scraps were left. But Willow kept that thought to herself. The truth was it *was* a useful skill. She was realising that now more than ever, when she couldn't access it like she used to. Truth be told, she missed her powers. It felt like a part of her was gone, and it made her feel odd.

'What do you do?' said Sprig to the wizard, who explained about his acquired ability – turning things to copper – and his old one, which hadn't been that much fun – his clouded eye.

Sprig grinned. 'So that's how this happened,' he

said, looking around at the copper bath-boat. 'It's a nice talent. Sorry it came at such a high price.'

'That's life, son,' said the wizard. 'We all pay a price, one way or another. Choosing to make it worth the price – that's what makes the difference.'

The boy nodded. 'Maybe you're right.'

Willow spent a restless night worrying about Nolin Sometimes and Moreg Vaine. The witch had to have had a reason for sending her Whisper. Willow wished that she'd just sent her a message instead. Did Moreg know who had taken Sometimes? Couldn't she have given her some idea of what to do?

In the morning, there were deep shadows beneath Willow's eyes as she prepared to leave.

The old wizard pulled her to one side and gave her a bear hug. 'I'm going to miss you, young Willow, and you too, Oswin,' he said, reaching down to pat the kobold's head, which was currently poking out of the hairy carpetbag.

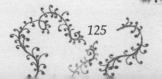

There was the sound of soft purring, followed by the sound of a throat being cleared. Oswin muttered, **'Fanks,'** and shot back inside the bag.

The wizard's lips twitched in amusement. He looked over Willow's shoulder, checking to see they were alone. Then he pressed something into her hands. It was the harmonica, which gave a soft hoot. Willow stared at it in surprise.

'I want ya to have this. It's old magic. It was once a part of the boat – a bit of extra metal I had left over when I made it. But the two are linked, like it's part of the same body, with one heart, if ya know what I mean?' Willow didn't, so he explained further. 'If ya blow on it, the boat will know, and if ya need me then I'll come.'

She blinked. 'You'd do that?'

He clamped a hand on her shoulder, making her knees buckle slightly. 'Course I will, lass.'

She grinned. There was a sound from behind, and she turned to find Sprig standing there. 'Thanks for bringing me Whisper.'

'Maybe we'll see each other again,' said Sprig.

'That would be nice,' she replied, her ears reddening slightly. Then she climbed on to the broomstick, placing the carpetbag at the end, and launched herself up into the air.

The sounds of Oswin's panicked cries of, 'Oh nOoo, NOT this **blooming** feathered flying sticks again!' grew in volume as they made their way towards the burgundy dawn sky.

11

Oh, Brother

As Willow flew, she saw a raven circle overhead. It gave a haunting cry, as if it were saying a last goodbye, and then it was gone, faster than she could blink.

Holloway had given her a rough map so that she could find her way to Wisperia. She squinted at the tiny scrawled diagram with the wizard's rather illegible writing, and the broom jerked around wildly, making Oswin's cries get even louder – if that were possible.

'*Oh NOOOO!*'

'Sorry, Os,' she said, quickly shoving the map back into her pocket and steadying the broom. They were heading the right way at least.

They flew for over an hour until there was a sudden rumble of thunder, followed by the light tickle of rain that soon turned into a heavy downpour. Willow huddled against the broomstick. The wind was icy and blowing hard, and water dripped down her nose, making it increasingly difficult to see.

When the water started creeping down her neck, making her shiver uncontrollably, she shook her head. *'I'm g-g-going t-t-o have to l-l-and.'*

'Prober belly,' was Oswin's reply from within the dry carpetbag.

Teeth chattering, Willow pointed her broomstick down towards a town near the winding river.

She landed just outside the town walls under an increasingly heavy downpour of rain, her hair clinging to her face in long, wet hanks. She climbed off Whisper with some difficulty, her hands frozen and claw-like from their grip.

'We'll *t-t-try* and find somewhere warm and *d-dry*,' she said with a shiver as she hunched against the rain.

In her hands, the carpetbag began to shake, and there was the familiar sound of Oswin's panicked wailings. *'Oh nooooo! Oh, me greedy aunt! Oh, Osbertrude, why'd yew 'ave ter curse us kobolds?'*

Willow could understand his distress, as up ahead

a band of men in familiar long brown-and-gold robes began to race towards her. *The Brothers of Wol.*

Willow's heart stuttered in her chest. She hadn't had a run-in with the Brothers since she had infiltrated their fortress, Wolkana, to get back the missing day.

One of them pointed and shouted, 'Witch! Attempting to enter a Forbidden area! Seize her!'

Willow didn't have time to think. She jumped back on Whisper and hurtled away, dodging an arrow that missed her by inches.

She swallowed, barely able to see in the stinging rain. Forbidden areas were enforced by the Brothers.

Parts of Starfell were off limits to magical people, as part of the treaty that was meant to keep the peace between magical and non-magical folk. However, it only seemed to be making things worse.

Another arrow shot past her, grazing her cheek. **'Oh no!'** cried Oswin.

Willow gulped as more and more arrows rained down on her. She couldn't see properly in the gloom, and she was forced to veer to the left as a tree branch nearly whacked her over the head. At that moment, a strange, haunting cry pierced the gloom. She cried out as a raven with a smoky blue-black wing flew in front of her.

There was a low gasp from within the bag. '*OH NO, OH NOOOOOOOOO . . . OH, ME GREEDY AUNT, A CURSE UPON YEH! I'M GONNA DIE AND ME LAST MEAL WILL 'AVE BEEN 'ORRID FRIED FISH! 'TIS NOT HOW A KOBOLD DESERVES TER GO!*'

Willow's heart thundered in her ears as Sprig chased her to the right, just in time to avoid an arrow that had been heading straight for her.

'Sprig!' she shouted as she watched the raven swoop down. Had he been hit?

She pointed her broom to follow him, her heart in her throat.

The wind was a mighty beast, and before she knew it they had crash-landed into a large, muddy patch, the carpetbag rolling off with a thud. She jumped up to find Sprig, but she couldn't see anything much in the gloom. 'Dear Wol! Sprig? Are you all right? Please, please be all right!'

She heard a rustling noise and the sound of a low moan. Then, 'I'm okay. It only grazed me. Just winded.'

Willow felt her knees give out.

There was a huff from within the carpetbag. '**I's fine too, fanks fer** asking.'

The boy gave a chuckle and Willow couldn't help grinning despite everything.

The kobold peered out of the carpetbag as the rain eased. **'Did you follow us?'** he demanded, his lamp-like eyes narrowing.

Sprig turned to look at Oswin and his face coloured slightly. 'Um, yes . . . I thought, I dunno, maybe I could help. I felt like I should have offered on the boat. I mean . . .' He cleared his throat, then glanced up at Willow. 'It's not every day someone says they're heading to Wisperia. I just felt – I don't know – responsible somehow.'

Willow shook her head. 'Why? I was always going to go. You bringing me Whisper just makes it a bit easier.'

He looked at her with his solemn black eyes. 'Nothing about Wisperia is easy. Besides, I felt bad that the witch left you to go after your friend alone.'

Despite how cold Willow was, she felt something warm creep inside her. 'Thank you.'

He gave her a small, shy smile.

Oswin crossed his arms, muttering darkly to himself that it seemed a bit odd that he wanted to come . . .

Willow decided to ignore him as she picked up the carpetbag. 'Will you be all right to fly?' she asked Sprig.

In answer, his body shuddered and he transformed back into a raven, flying to perch on the back of her broom.

Willow peered up at the sky and saw the gloom was clearing, and there was no further sign of arrows.

As the sun rose higher, they flew up towards its warmth. She managed to dry out somewhat as they made their way past winding rivers, and the floating Cloud Mountains, towards the most dangerous and beautiful forest Willow had ever known.

Wisperia.

12

The Iris Inside the Jar

Wisperia was even more magnificent than Willow remembered. Impossibly vast, the multicoloured forest stretched for miles, as far as the eye could see.

Perhaps it was seeing it from her broomstick, and therefore going more slowly than she had been when she first saw the forest from the back of Feathering, but Willow felt like she could take in more this time than she had in between the rapid wingbeats of the dragon.

There were strange birds with translucent wings that appeared to have been created out of bright turquoise and cerise watercolour ink. There were wind monkeys with white fur and orange spots down their backs, and purple deer with blue tails. Trees grew in every colour imaginable, with electric leaves of pink and blue and purple.

In the canopy, dotted here and there, Willow spotted small communities that wound round the vast trees.

'Oh, *me* 'ORRID *aunt*, where's *me* stove?' whispered Oswin, peering out at the scene, his eyes creeping above the top of the hairy bag in absolute horror.

Her eyes widened as she saw elves with blue skin, bows and arrows on their backs as they hunted among the trees. There were wood sprites, who looked like they were made of green smoke, dashing up the colourful bark. Their laughter was loud as they gathered fruit and nuts in heavy woven baskets, which they transported up the network of trees so fast it was impossible to see how they did it.

There were people going about their day, making tools, preparing food and walking or flying as they chatted in groups – though they weren't like any people Willow had ever seen before. They were the ones she'd been told about, with leaves for fingers or flames for hair, hooves for feet . . . and WINGS. They were the ones who'd been transformed by the wild magic of the forest.

'I never saw them when I was here before,' she breathed, eyes wide as they flew over one of the treetop villages. She stared down at the treehouses, which were shaped like vast teardrops, intricately made from electric-coloured vines. Some were brightest pink while others were vivid blue or green or brilliant white. They dangled from the branches like strange, beautiful birdcages.

'The last time I was here, we flew high, way above the canopy, towards the Great Wisperia Tree. I never saw this,' she exhaled.

The broomstick shuddered and dipped as Sprig turned back into a boy. Willow twisted round to look at him as he said, 'It's here, closer to the ground, that you see what Wisperia is really like.'

'Have you spent time here?' she asked in surprise.

'Some,' he acknowledged. 'Mostly as a raven. The magic doesn't really affect me much when I'm in bird form – can't speak as a bird either,' he added, explaining the reason he had transformed back into a boy. 'They're really interesting, the people here. They don't talk like us; they communicate like birds, in song. It's their own language, though only the forest-touched can understand it.'

Willow's eyes widened at this. As they flew, they passed a group of what looked like children perching

on top of a branch. They all had different-coloured leaves for hair and arms, from turquoise to bright pink, gold and flame-orange. As she stared, they jumped off the branch, their leaf-like arms acting as wings. Keeping pace with Willow's broom, they turned and spiralled, each attempting to outdo the other as they performed beautiful aerial displays, which Willow realised were for their benefit. There was a sound almost like laughter as she clapped at their colourful display, then they turned and headed back, something like birdsong sounding sweetly in the air.

'What was that about?' breathed Willow in wonder.

Sprig shrugged. 'I think they're just as curious about you as you are about them. Not many regular folk come to Wisperia, see. The young ones haven't learnt to be fearful of outsiders yet.'

Sprig's words made her frown slightly, despite her delight at the youngsters' antics. She supposed not everyone who came to Wisperia was kind to those they deemed different to them.

As the afternoon wore on, they flew towards the heart of the enormous, colourful forest, where a giant pale tree the colour of blue sea glass dominated the landscape. It was the Great Wisperia Tree, where, up at the very top, Nolin Sometimes's house perched on stilts, swaying gently in the wind.

There were rocks suspended in the air that made a ladder up to the house, and everywhere there were strange plants in teapots, some with fur or hair or eyes.

Willow made for the porch, and left Whisper outside propped up against the railing.

It felt strange to be here without Sometimes to welcome them. She noticed that without him the rocks and lanterns that usually lit up outside his stilt house weren't illuminated, and couldn't help feeling his absence more than ever.

She opened the door to the sound of snoring. There was a faint '*Oh, OSBERTRUDE, oh, me 'orrid aunt, I forgot about 'im!*' from the carpetbag.

The snoring stopped as their footsteps sounded at the entrance. From the cluttered wooden desk near the door there was a loud humming sound.

'The furlarms,' Willow remembered, coming forward to touch one of the funny, hairy creatures. It stopped humming at her touch, only to look at her balefully.

Abruptly, something heavy and large hit the floor, and Willow turned to find that Harold, a large brown dog with lots of wrinkly skin and a long, lolling tongue, had jumped off the bed by the window. He yelped excitedly to see them, and Willow bent down to give the dog a scratch and a cuddle, to Oswin's harrumph of annoyance.

'Sorry, Harold, it's just us,' she said as the dog moved on quickly from them to the door. He stared out hopefully for Sometimes's return, then howled softly when he realised he wasn't coming.

Willow's heart sank. She felt terrible for him. 'That's why we're here. We're going to try and get him back.'

'I don't think he understands that,' said Sprig, looking at the dog, then grinning at her.

Willow nodded, but couldn't bring herself to return his smile. It was all too sad being here without Sometimes. 'I'll check around in here,' she said, and Sprig suggested he look outside for any signs of who had taken Sometimes.

Willow started with the small kitchen in the corner, filled with yellow cupboards and hundreds of teapots, looking for signs of a struggle, hoping that there would be some clue left behind.

The only thing she could find was the back door open, slamming against the wind. On the mat, there was a faint scuffmark, and a plant that looked like it had been crushed, perhaps from Sometimes's hasty departure. She knelt down to pick it up and a tiny plant frond seemed to lift itself towards her before it stopped moving.

Willow bit her lip. The plants Nolin Sometimes collected always seemed somehow more alive, more unusual. She took it to the kitchen and let it stand in a small saucer of water, hoping that would revive it – though she doubted it sadly. Sometimes would know what to do for it.

Her chest felt heavy as she carried on searching through the rest of the treehouse. Whenever she felt this way, like there was no hope left, she saw Granny Flossy's face. She closed her eyes and shook the image away, a tear forming at the corner of her eye. What if she didn't find Sometimes? Would she lose him too?

A noise made her turn. Sprig had returned. 'I couldn't see anything outside in the garden – no telltale signs. I think they must have caught him while he was running away.'

Willow nodded. That's what she thought too, her heart sinking as if a lead weight had pushed it down to her toes. She turned away to dab at her eyes surreptitiously. She walked back towards the large, cluttered desk near the front door, where the furlarms were sitting quietly. It was strewn with an array of plants in jam jars, dried leaves, botanical sketches and feathers. Night was beginning to fall, and it was growing ever darker in the treehouse.

Where was he? Who had wanted to take him and why?

She picked up notebooks and feathers, unable to speak past the lump forming in her throat.

Suddenly there was a loud pop, and Oswin cried, **'Oi, wot 'appened to the sofa?'**

Willow blinked, her heart starting to race. Had she made it disappear?

Oswin's head peeped out of the bag, and his fur went from orange to green as he saw her face fall. He lifted his paws out as if to stop her as she began to breathe heavily. **'*Oh no,*'** he whispered.

Sprig found a box of matches and some candles in the kitchen and brought them over, not noticing her distress as he muttered, 'These should give us some

light. I was thinking we could rustle up something for dinner, then first thing tomorrow we'll have a look at the trail. I have his scent now.' He lifted up one of Nolin Sometimes's discarded jumpers. 'This should help.'

Then, catching sight of Oswin's wide, panicked eyes and the way his ears were flattened to his skull, Sprig blinked. 'What – what is it?'

He turned to look at Willow, whose lip trembled. She clutched at her chest, but it was like no air could fill her lungs. Suddenly the desk vanished with a loud pop, and Sprig jumped back just in time as everything that had been on it plummeted to the flagstone floor with an almighty

CRASH.

The kobold dived out of the carpetbag and ran towards Willow's legs. He clung to them with his paws, shaking, his huge, lamp-like eyes beseeching hers. **'Jes stop it – it 'appens when yer upset! Calm yerself!'**

Willow's heart was beating fast, there were spots in front of her eyes, and there were more and more popping sounds as things continued to disappear.

'I don't KNOW HOW!'

Sprig came to stand in front of her and placed his hands on her shoulders, his face inches from hers. 'Look at me,' he commanded, and in her panic she did, focusing on his dark eyes. 'Close your eyes! Do it.'

Willow did.

'Now, deep breath in,' he said.

'W-what, I – I—' tried Willow, who wasn't really hearing him beyond the roaring in her ears.

'Listen to 'im,' beseeched Oswin, tapping her leg.

Willow swallowed, then took a deep breath in.

'Good,' said Sprig. 'And let it out. Now, as you breathe in again, count to ten.'

She did as he said.

He counted out loud. 'Now breathe out.'

Her breath came rushing out. 'I-I – er,' she

stammered, opening her eyes. 'I don't know what that—'

'Close your eyes and do it again. Breathe in, counting to ten.'

She did.

'Again. Just trust me, keep going. You'll feel it soon.'

Willow did it four more times, then, at last, felt her heartbeat begin to slow.

'Keep taking deep breaths. Don't open your eyes.'

Willow nodded. After a few minutes, she was almost back to normal. Sprig's hands on her shoulders were cold yet somehow reassuring. When she opened her eyes at last, it was like all the colour and warmth of the treehouse was there to greet her, somehow more full of life than it had been.

'*Yew* **all** *right?*' whispered the kobold.

Willow felt embarrassed, but nodded.

'I used to get attacks like that – the only thing that helped was the breathing,' said Sprig.

'Thanks,' she said softly, 'for helping me.'

He shrugged. 'Sure. If you don't mind me asking . . . what was that about?' he said, pointing to where the desk had been.

Willow told him a bit about what had happened to her magic lately. His eyes widened. 'I've never heard of magic being scrambled like that.'

'Yeah,' said Willow.

She thought of Holloway's words. *'There's only one thing I've ever known that can do that to a person. Grief.'*

She looked away and made a show of trying to pick up all the things that had fallen on to the floor. The furlarms, in particular, were glaring at her with reproachful eyes. As she considered them, she tried not to think about Granny Flossy. She couldn't afford to fall apart – not now, not when her friend needed her. She felt a twist of shame, and anger at herself. Why couldn't her magic just simply work?

'I've got this, it's okay,' said Willow as Sprig bent down to help her.

Perhaps he sensed that she wanted to be alone because he suggested that the kobold help him with dinner. 'C'mon, Oswin, there are some apple-pie blossoms we can pick from the branches outside, and we can see what's left in the cupboards.'

Oswin, who had been making his way quietly back

to his carpetbag, stopped and turned round in shock. **'Wot?'** He'd never really been asked to do any chores before.

Willow felt the ghost of a smile flit across her face at his horrified expression.

The cluttered contents of Sometimes's desk had made an incredible mess and Willow had barely scratched the surface of her clean-up when Sprig returned with their simple dinner of apple-pie blossoms and dried penji berries. Sprig offered to help Willow clean up again, but she declined, and shortly afterwards she could hear the sound of his and Oswin's snores coming from the sofa that had reappeared during their meal.

It had been a rather long day, but Willow was too keyed up to sleep, too distracted by her worry for Sometimes. She picked up the scattered feathers, plants and botanical prints and drawings that had fallen from the desk when it vanished. Thankfully, the desk had reappeared shortly afterwards. She'd made such a mess. While it was technically an accident, as she couldn't control what was happening to her powers, she couldn't help feeling terrible about it. She was meant to be finding Sometimes, but all her abilities seemed to be doing now was making things worse. These were his observations, his studies on the strange plants that lived in Wisperia and their hidden magical abilities. She was determined to put everything right.

Thankfully, though a few empty jars had broken, the rest had been protected somehow. Each one had a little label, and the roots of the plants inside them grew in water, soil, or just in air. Willow noticed one plant with hairy green leaves and a sharp, knife-edged stamen the colour of blood. Its label, written in Nolin Sometimes's messy scrawl, said,

The carvery, one of the most dangerous plants in the world, causes paralysis in the area it stabs for up to a year. Handle with caution, wear gloves.

She put it on the ground fast and righted another. Inside the jar were wispy yellow and pink tendrils that swirled to form what looked like a dress that was dancing. Willow found it hard to look away as it moved, and her mind went pleasingly blank as she watched it sway. Music, as if from nowhere, started to hum in

her ears, until a loud snore from Harold jerked her out of her reverie. She read the plant's specimen label:

The enchantress. Known to hypnotise whoever looks at it, useful for immobilising an intruder.

She blinked. Some of these were a bit *dangerous*, she realised. Not quite the types of plants she remembered Sometimes showing her in his moon garden. Still, she couldn't help being fascinated by them. Part of her looked out for some plant remedy that might help restore her magic, but she couldn't find anything in this collection, and, without knowing what the plants in his garden were, she didn't have much hope of finding a solution, not without Sometimes. Though she was beginning to suspect that Holloway had been right – that her magic was being scrambled by her grief – and she didn't know if there was cure for that at all . . . She swallowed, trying to push the hopeless feeling away.

Gradually, Willow organised all of Sometimes's papers and righted all the plants, finding some that had rolled under the bed beside the sleeping dog.

The last thing she picked up was a small jam jar, inside which was a purple, iris-like flower with long, thin, dark blue roots suspended in the air. As she touched the glass, the plant appeared to wilt slightly, petals hunched over, reminding her a little of a grumbling Gertrude, which sulked when it wasn't watered. Without really thinking, Willow fetched a glass of water from the kitchen and trickled some into the jar. To her surprise, when she put the lid back on, the plant seemed to wiggle, perhaps in satisfaction. It began to shimmer, turning into an almost smoke-like substance that was iridescent like glitter, dark purple threaded with blue.

As Willow touched the glass, the smoke-like substance followed her finger and started to shift as it formed itself into a young girl with long, stick-straight hair and a misshapen dress with a haphazardly sewn hem. The girl was pointing a finger at the glass. It was like looking into a small mirror made of purple shadows.

Willow swallowed. Something about it gave her the creeps.

Her eye drifted to the small label, but, instead of finding an explanation of what this plant was,

Willow's creeped-out feeling intensified. As it wasn't a label at all.

It said:

MP for Willow Moss.

It was a clue.

13

Feathering's Return

Willow stared at her shadow miniature in the jam jar for some time. Every now and again, it seemed to shudder slightly. When she took her finger away, the smoke-like shadows shifted and turned once more into a purple iris with long, thin roots suspended in the air.

Why would Nolin Sometimes have left her this? What was it supposed to tell her?

Willow went to sit in the armchair by the window to think. But at some point she must have nodded off, despite herself, because suddenly there was a small flash of light, and Willow blinked awake. On the floor was the leaf-scroll. It was the message that had gone missing from her attic before she ran away from home! Surprised, she bent down to pick it up when suddenly the sound of the furlarms began to whine loudly throughout the treehouse.

'**Oh no!**' cried Oswin as she dashed towards them. Harold started to howl as well.

'What is it?' asked Sprig, starting awake too, his dark eyes wary yet sharp as he looked around in alarm.

'I don't know,' whispered Willow, fear clutching at her throat. 'The furlarms detect intruders, though.'

She looked up towards the window with a worried frown and saw something large, like a cloud, heading straight towards them in a sky that was turning pink with the dawn.

'Maybe it's whoever came for Sometimes . . . Maybe they're coming back,' breathed Willow, looking worried.

'*Oh*, ***Osbertrude***, *a curse upon* ***yeh***, *me* ***greedy*** *aunt!*' whispered Oswin, who'd climbed on to the armchair to see out of the window better.

Whatever was moving towards them at breakneck speed sparkled in the early-morning sunshine with a pearly blue glow, and Willow's fear suddenly changed to delight.

'It's Feathering!' she cried.

'Feathering?' asked Sprig, his eyes widening in

sudden fear as the blueish cloud neared. He took a step back from the window, his outline seeming to shift from boy to raven then back to boy so fast it hurt her eyes. 'Is that A DRAGON?'

'Yes! C'mon,' she said, pulling him along by his arm. 'This is the best news – maybe he knows who's taken Sometimes!'

Willow raced outside towards a large branch the width of a road, with Sprig following more slowly behind her. As the dragon came in to land, the force blew Willow's hair back and she clutched on to a nearby branch.

'Why, hello there, young Willow. We wondered if we would find you here,' said Feathering in his deep, wind-rattling-a-window voice.

Willow dashed forward to greet the dragon, and saw to her surprise that Essential Jones, another of her friends who had helped to save the missing day, was on his back. A grin split her face as Essential jumped down.

'Hi, Willow!' the girl said with a big smile, pushing back her glasses. Her long dark hair was like a knotty helmet around her head, and her nut-coloured skin

seemed to glow with health and excitement from the ride.

'Feathering! Essential! It's wonderful to see you,' cried Willow, racing forward to hug Essential and pat the dragon's snout. Feathering's golden eye closed slightly in pleasure at seeing her, and then widened as it took in the boy, who was lagging in the shadows behind her.

'And who's this?' he asked, showing a row of perfect white teeth.

'This is Sprig.'

The dragon sniffed the air, then he blinked. His head snapped up fast, making Willow and Essential leap back. The gentle giant she knew suddenly looked fierce, the iris in his golden eye whirling in a strange way that made her heart start to pound. In a rather cold voice, he said, 'If you *take* her, I will come for you.'

There were goose pimples all along Willow's body.

Sprig had turned pale. 'H-how did you know—' he started.

'I can always smell death, boy . . .'

Willow frowned, then shot a look at Sprig. 'What?'

'I mean no harm,' said Sprig, raising his arms.

'See that you keep it that way,' warned the dragon.

Willow blinked. 'Death? What are you talking about?'

Sprig kept a wary eye on Feathering. 'There's something you should know about how I was born . . .'

'More a question of *where*,' emphasised the cloud dragon. Feathering sniffed the air, his golden eye falling on the boy's arm, the one that was blue and black and scored with concentric circles. Sprig pulled his jumper sleeve down.

'Where were you born?' asked Willow.

Sprig looked down for a moment. 'I . . . I was born on the edge of the Mists . . .'

Essential frowned. 'Mists?' she asked.

'The Mists of Mitlaire.'

Willow and Essential gasped.

Sprig nodded. 'Yes. Umbellifer tried to claim me, but I was pulled back in time, so only my arm was touched by death. But it's like having a foot in both worlds. I can travel through the Mists and into Netherfell without, you know . . .'

'Losing your soul?' said Willow with a blink.

Essential's eyes widened.

'Yes.' He ran a hand through his hair, shooting the dragon a wary glance. Then he looked at Willow, beseeching her with his solemn black eyes. 'People think it's creepy, so I don't always tell them the truth about where I'm from . . .'

Willow blew out the air in her lungs. She thought of how much Sprig had helped her – how he'd risked his life against the Brothers of Wol and their arrows to save her, and how he had calmed her when she was overwhelmed.

'Sprig wouldn't harm me, Feathering,' she said. 'You can trust him.' She looked at the boy, wishing he'd told her about this earlier, but she didn't want to say anything while they were around the others. She supposed she could understand him not saying anything if this was how some people reacted.

The dragon didn't respond, and Willow took a deep breath. The truth was they had other things to worry about – they had a dear friend who needed them. 'Feathering, have you heard – is that why you're here? About Sometimes?'

Essential and Feathering looked confused.

'Why, what's happened?' asked Essential.

Willow sighed. She'd been hoping that maybe they knew something. 'It's really bad. Nolin Sometimes was captured!'

Essential gasped.

The dragon's eye swivelled to Willow, his reservations about Sprig momentarily forgotten. 'CAPTURED? By whom?' he breathed.

'I don't know! He asked me to help him – and I've been trying – but m-my magic has failed. I came here because he asked me to look in on Harold and I've—'

'So that's why you're here!' gasped Essential. 'Everyone was worried about you.'

'About me?' asked Willow. It was her turn to be surprised.

Essential nodded, pushing her glasses up her nose. 'Yes, it's been mad – your mother sent a message to Rubix, asking her to keep an eye out for you as you'd run away. So I persuaded Rubix to go and see them, as I was worried. But it was so strange – because of the missing day, none of them remembered that you and I had met before. They were asking all kinds of questions. Panicking, I think. That's why I'm so relieved you're here. I don't know if you've heard about the Brothers of Wol?'

Willow blinked, then looked from Sprig to Essential. 'Heard what?' She felt uneasy. They may have succeeded in restoring the stolen day, but she was sure that the trouble in Wolkana was not over.

Silas, the Brother who had stolen the day, was still out there, and she was sure he must be furious. She didn't know what he was planning now . . .

'There's some new edict they signed,' said Essential. 'It's horrible – now they can lock up any witch or wizard they believe may be a threat. It was meant to be only if they were acting dangerously, but the Brothers of Wol have taken it to mean all powerful magical people. Magic folk are saying that they've broken the treaty – things are not looking good.'

Willow gasped. 'No! That's horrible! I had no idea.'

Essential nodded. 'I'm so glad they didn't take you! Your mother was worried that you might have been captured. That's why I came – and I met Feathering on the way. I thought if you'd run away there was probably a good reason.' She pushed up her glasses again and gave her a grin, which Willow returned. She couldn't help feeling so grateful for her friends.

'Thank you,' said Willow, who felt a stab of guilt at making them all worry, especially her family. 'You were right. I had to leave – they wouldn't believe me. They didn't trust that Sometimes was missing. See, I got this note from him.' She showed them the leaf-scroll that had recently reappeared.

'Oh no!' cried Essential. 'This is terrible!'

Feathering's golden eye widened as he read it. He shook his head. 'I had a feeling something was wrong. I came across one of the rock dragons – they stay dormant for years in the Cloud Mountains, but one of them woke up when a pepper tree kept calling for me and making the rock dragon sneeze. By the time I got there, though, the pepper tree had long since walked off.' He sighed, then added, 'It was a bit bruised. Rock dragons, you know . . . not exactly gentle beasts.'

Willow did *not* know. She hadn't even known there were such things as *rock dragons*. But what Feathering said made sense. 'Sometimes mentioned in the letter that he tried to contact you.' She read the bit about 'pepper-tree communication' again.

Feathering nodded. 'Yes, he planted it a few weeks ago when he came for a visit. It was a nice gesture, as he knows how fond I am of pepper tea. He mentioned something about being able to stay in touch, but I didn't think anything of it. I assumed he meant he'd just be coming round more often – I didn't realise he had the skill to communicate with the tree's spirit.'

Essential's eyes widened. 'Well, it is pretty rare . . .'

Willow nodded, thinking about the oak tree in her

garden that Sometimes had used to contact her in the same way.

Feathering looked sad. 'What a pity the tree missed me. Perhaps this could have been prevented if I'd been home. Was it them, the Brothers of Wol? Did they come for him because he's a danger?'

Willow shook her head. 'I don't know. But how is he a danger, out here away from everyone?'

They shrugged. It didn't make sense – Sometimes was more of a danger around others, blurting out their memories and secrets. There was more reason to leave him miles away from people than to capture him . . .

Then Willow smacked her forehead. In the excitement of Feathering's arrival, she'd almost forgotten. 'Hang on, there's something else. I found it before you came,' she said, then raced back inside the stilt house to fetch the plant that had been addressed to her. She skipped back again over the suspended rocks and showed them the strange iris in the jam jar.

'MP?' asked Essential, her eyes scanning the label. 'What does that mean?'

Willow shrugged. 'I don't know. Most of the plants inside have labels saying what they are, except for a few, so it looks like maybe he hadn't got round to filling them all out. Do you think it means something?'

'It might just have been something he cultivated for you, something that reminded him of you,' said Feathering. 'He planted the pepper tree on the mountain for me because he knew I liked the tea.'

Willow's heart sank at the dragon's words.

Sprig ran a hand through his dark hair. He looked thin and solemn next to the dragon, who still clearly didn't trust him. 'I think it's a clue,' he said to their surprise. 'He is smart, from all you've said. Also, I agree it's unlikely to have been the Brothers.'

Willow frowned, then looked back at the jam jar in the palm of her hand. The plant seemed to flicker in the light for a moment. 'Maybe Sprig is right. Like you said, Feathering, not much grows on the Cloud Mountains, and Sometimes knew that if he planted that tree he could use it to try and get in touch with you. So maybe it was a bit of both – something you liked, but also something he could use to contact you if needed . . .'

'That's true,' the dragon acknowledged. 'It did bring me here.'

Essential peered at the note from Sometimes that was still in her hands, then frowned. Her fingers touched the little splodge at the end that looked like a plant doodle. 'It's an *iris*!' she breathed. Then she showed it to Willow and the others. 'He wanted you to find this, look!'

They stared at the note in Essential's hands. 'You're right!' cried Willow.

'Maybe he couldn't tell you what he'd left for you in case whoever had taken him saw it – but he knows that you understand his connection with plants. Maybe he trusted that you'd work out what this means?' suggested Essential.

Feathering nodded. 'I think so too.'

'But how will we find out what it is?' asked Sprig. 'Is there another forgotten teller we can ask?

'No, they're really rare,' sighed Essential.

Willow nodded. 'And extremely hard to find.'

She pulled out the StoryPass. The needle went from '*There be Dragons*' to '*One Might Have Suspected as Such*'. She tested its heavy brass weight in her palm, then she frowned as she considered the compass-like device. It hadn't given her an answer, but it did give her an idea of where

they might look for one.

'We might not be able to track down any other forgotten tellers,' she said, 'but I think I know another way we can find out what this plant is . . . My friend Holloway said that there's a place you could go to if you needed to learn something – where all the magical secrets of Starfell are kept. *Library.* I think

that's where

we have

to go.'

14

Capture

'It's worth trying,' said Sprig. 'If anyone would know, I think it would be the people of Library.'

The dragon stared at him. 'I will take Willow and Essential. You may follow behind us, *raven.*'

'Feathering!' Willow exclaimed, surprised. She had never known him to be rude.

Sprig shook his head. 'It's fine, Willow. I'm happy to follow.'

Willow nodded. 'Well, I'll just go and fetch my broom then.' She grinned. 'And Oswin. I think he'll be happy to see you both.'

'Oh yes,' said Essential, who was rather fond of Oswin.

There was a tinkly peal of laughter, like wind chimes. 'I doubt that he feels that way about me,' said Feathering, 'but I shall be glad to see the kobold in any case.'

'*Oh noooooo*, not that great blooming *feathered* beast *again! Wot yew go and signs us ups for this time?*' moaned Oswin as Willow helped him back into the green hairy bag, where she had also put the leaf-scroll and the jam jar plant. Oswin, it had to be said, didn't much like to come out in daylight, and had risked staying indoors with Harold again rather than venturing out into the wind.

'Shh,' she said. 'We're off to Library.' And she filled him in on what had happened.

Oswin groaned. '**Oh no,** anywhere **but there!**'

'Why? What do you mean?'

'Jes yew waits. It's '**orrible. Dusty. B**ooks everywheres. I **got** lost there once ... worst thing *ever.*'

'What happened?'

'I **don**' wanna talk **about** it,' he said, then zipped himself into the bag. '**Lets me know when** we is leaving that **infermerol** place.'

'All right,' said Willow, her lips twitching.

Harold had gone back to sleep. She felt bad leaving him behind all by himself – they hadn't been here for that long. But at least they'd checked up on him as Sometimes had asked. She turned to leave, picking up

the bag and collecting Whisper on the way out, and made her way to Feathering, Essential and Sprig, who had already transformed into a raven.

She climbed on to the dragon, and Essential got on behind her. Willow felt her stomach plummet to the ground as Feathering leapt off the tree and launched himself up high into the clouds.

They flew over the Great Wisperia Tree, where she could see Sometimes's moon garden, and down below, in the canopy of strange-coloured trees, birds of all shapes, sizes and colours went past. They made Sprig's stark black feathers stand out as he kept pace with Feathering.

The dragon shot the raven a dark look that Willow couldn't help noticing.

'Why don't you like Sprig? I don't get it,' she asked, leaning close to his ear.

'**Wells, since yew asks _finally_ ... not like yew gave me much choice on 'is company or not . . .**

but 'e's weird . . . **Somefink** about 'im, I dunno, jes gave **me** the creeps. Also 'e changes into a huntings bird which tries **ter go** after fluffy-looking prey like me,' huffed Oswin from the carpetbag.

Willow looked at the bag and hid a snort. 'Thank you, *Oswin*. I didn't know that. I doubt, though, that Sprig will eat you. And I was asking Feathering actually.'

The dragon seemed to laugh in his wind-chime way, and then he paused and sighed. 'It's not a question of "like", Willow. The kobold is right – the boy is strange. I'm just advising caution.'

Willow frowned. *Strange.* That wasn't a good enough reason as far as she was concerned. It felt wrong to mistrust someone just because they were a little different. Wasn't that exactly how non-magical people treated magic folk?

Most people thought of Willow as odd, but it didn't give them the right to treat her differently. Sprig might be unusual, but he was trying to help. Look at how he'd saved her from the Brothers of Wol. She frowned. They would see that he meant well.

Essential squeezed her shoulder. 'I thought he seemed nice.'

Willow turned to her and smiled.

There was a snort from the bag about 'hags not 'aving much sense when it comes to boys.'

The sound of birdsong interrupted Willow's thoughts, and she recalled the forest-touched children from the treetop community who had followed them the day before. But when Oswin's panicked wailings of 'Oh NO, oh, me greedy aunt Osbertrude!' reached a deafening crescendo, she twisted round to look and her eyes widened in shock.

These were not children. Before she could blink, they were surrounded by two dozen flying creatures of all shapes and sizes. There were the people with flames for hair, and others with leaves for fingers. There were blue elves and green sprites and wind monkeys, and others that were stranger still, almost as big as the dragon, with horns coming out of their heads, hooves for feet and huge wings. They were all advancing on them fast, with fierce, menacing eyes, some with nostrils flared and others with bows and arrows at the ready.

Willow swallowed. '*Oh no*' indeed.

15

Forest-touched

Before Willow could gather enough air in her lungs to scream, several of the creatures flew at Feathering.

Willow's heart started to beat rapidly, and the next thing she knew she was being snatched away by what looked like a woman who was part elk – with large, twisted, dark blue horns on her head and hooves for feet – and part something else entirely, as she had giant blue-green wings.

Willow screamed as she thrashed against the strong horned woman's grip. 'LET ME GO!'

She watched in horror as Essential and Sprig found themselves in similar dire straits, Essential dragged off in a net of leaves by one of the leaf-people, and Sprig whisked away by an elf with fierce yellow eyes and a powerful-looking bow.

Feathering roared his fury. 'What is the meaning of this? Who DARES to attack a dragon?' His wind-chime voice had turned to the angry howl of a storm, loud and fearsome above the forest. Birds flew in all directions at the noise.

Still the creatures wrestled him from the sky. Willow noticed that one of them, a towering man with midnight skin and green flames for hair, seemed to be flying without the need for wings, powered somehow by air. Together with several wind monkeys and leaf-haired people, they threw what looked like a net made of purple branches over Feathering and dragged him towards the canopy below.

Willow felt her panic begin to mount as the horned woman followed after them. 'Where are you taking us? Stop it! *Leave us alone!'*

She could hear Oswin's similar wailings from the hairy green bag as he was carried away by a small wind monkey with white fur and transparent wings. **'Oh no! Get off me, yer hairy carbuncle!'**

They were carried to a treetop village where those strange, tear-shaped houses hung like odd birdcages, as jewel-bright as the forest itself. Willow and her friends were taken past these homes towards the very top of one of the trees, to a large, open, wooden structure shaped like a star. It looked a bit like a stage or a platform.

To Willow's relief, the horned woman with the large sea-green wings finally set her down, and she was joined shortly by Sprig and Essential, who were dropped with a thud in the centre of the platform.

Sprig flapped his wings in agitation. Essential's glasses were hanging off her nose. 'WHAT IS THIS ABOUT?' she demanded angrily, sitting up and throwing out a hand to freeze one of the wind monkeys who was trying to snatch her glasses. The freeze only lasted for a second, as Essential's ability wasn't very powerful, but she managed to keep her glasses nonetheless.

'Yes, tell us why you've taken us!' cried Willow.

The horned woman regarded them with piercing yellow eyes. '*Sekac moon?*' she said.

Willow was distracted, though, by another wind monkey, who had set Oswin down and was trying to pat the kobold through the bag. This wasn't going down very well. The monkey made a sound that sounded alarmingly like, '*Fat kitty . . .*'

'Oi, **stop** that! I is a **fearsome monster** – 'onestly, **peoples** jes 'ave **no** respect for kobolds these days. I is **NOT** a pet!'

Meanwhile, Feathering was fighting against the net they had thrown over him. The dragon vowed to eat them all, cloud dragon or no.

The man with midnight skin and flaming hair glared at him. '*Sekac,*' he said, like the horned woman.

It was a language Willow had never heard before, and she stared. 'I don't understand,' she said.

The horned woman took a step forward, and
Willow saw that her legs were bowed like a goat's,
strong and covered in thick blue-green hair. Her eyes
blazed. 'It is we who will ask questions first. You.
What are you doing in the forest? What did you want
from the tree?'

It sounded like she was not used to speaking their
language.

'The tree?' asked Essential, freezing the same wind
monkey who'd tried to take her glasses and was now
trying to touch her long, curly hair.

At Essential's question, several
of the forest creatures started
speaking rapidly in birdsong that
trilled loudly in their ears.

'The Great Tree,' said the
horned woman. 'We know you
were there. Don't lie to us,
child.'

Willow paled. 'My friend
lives there – at the top. He sent
me a letter, asking for my help.'
As Willow reached into her dress
pocket, there was more angry

179

birdsong. Willow wondered what that other language was that they spoke – was it part of the bird-like one, or was it something else?

'You will not use your magic on us!' said an older man with leaves for hair. 'It is forbidden in the *starjna*!'

Willow swallowed. She didn't know what he meant by *starjna*, but she held up her hands in a gesture of peace. 'I-I'm not using magic, I promise. It's just a leaf-scroll – it was from my friend.' Then she took the scroll from her pocket and showed it to them. 'See?'

The horned woman frowned, then stepped forward to take the letter from Willow. Her vast wings settled round her body like jewelled robes, winking in the morning light. They looked like stained-glass windows. A strange look came over her face as she touched the leaf-scroll, and the fire in her yellow eyes seemed to momentarily calm. She trilled something softly in the bird language and there was an answering hoot from one of the wind monkeys.

'My friend was captured,' Willow explained.

'Yes, we—' The horned woman broke off suddenly.

There were more angry warbles, and the man with the green flames for hair shot the horned woman a warning look as they seemed to discuss something in their strange bird language.

Sprig cocked his head to the side, almost as if he were trying to listen, but when Willow looked at him he lifted his blue-black wing as if to say he didn't understand.

Willow stared at the horned woman. 'Did you take him?'

Hope that he was near, and fear that he was in grave danger from these fierce creatures, filled her heart. Perhaps they didn't want him here in Wisperia. Maybe they thought of him as an outsider, not one of them – someone who was using the forest with his strange botany experiments . . . Perhaps he'd seen some of their secrets, and they didn't want a witness to them. Would they keep Willow and her friends here too? All of this and more raced through her whirling mind.

The horned woman shook her head. 'It was not us who took him. It was the—'

Suddenly there was an ear-splitting chorus of birdsong. The flame-haired man's voice was loudest, and he turned to glare at the horned woman. 'Know your place. Remember what you risk,' he said in Shel

– the common language of Starfell. Then he hissed something that sounded almost like '*merali*'.

The horned woman stepped back, dipping her head towards him, almost like a bow, then said nothing.

Willow stared, not understanding. What was that about? 'Do you know who took him? Did you see?'

The horned woman shook her head. 'We cannot say. It is not our way, I'm sorry.'

Willow stood up abruptly. They knew who had taken Nolin Sometimes, but wouldn't tell them? Anger and frustration bubbled up inside her. 'Why? Please, he needs us! If you know anything, you have to tell us. We're so worried about him – anything you know could help us find him. Please – he's our friend.'

The horned woman shook her head. 'This we cannot do. Beroc was right to remind me. It is *helia* – risking the lives of others, especially ones who are so young, is forbidden—'

'Pardon me, but I'd hazard that I am older than all of you combined!' huffed Feathering.

The horned woman gave him a rare smile and said, 'That would be the worst sort of *helia* – to risk a rare creature such as yourself. You cannot ask it of us.' Her eyes grew guarded again as she stepped back and repeated, 'Please do not ask me more of this. We will remember him, your friend. He was . . . strange, but one of us in many ways. We shall remember him when we say the blessings at the purple moon.'

Willow felt anger flush her face. They were speaking of him as if it were already too late! As if he were dead. As if they had given up all *hope*.

'B-but he's still alive – I'm sure of it! He doesn't need a – a – *blessing*! He needs our help! And you could give it, if he's your friend as you say! You don't have to risk *anything*, surely, in just *telling* us who took him?'

'No, that would be the worst thing we could do,' refused the horned woman. 'We are not afraid of the risk to us, but to you. We say this as a caution, not to be unkind: it is best if you leave it now.'

Willow frowned. She didn't understand these fierce magical people at all. They knew who'd taken Sometimes, but wouldn't give them any clues to find him, even though they claimed he was their friend and that they didn't want to be unkind!

Essential snorted. She seemed just as exasperated as Willow. 'Why did you take us then? What do you want from us?'

The horned woman looked sad. 'After the breach, we had to be sure of who entered our lands. We will protect the forest and fight intruders if we need to – but we won't start a war for a quarrel that isn't ours.'

Feathering looked confused. 'What breach? What quarrel?'

'I will say no more. However . . .' The horned woman turned and there was the sound of birdsong. One of the wind monkeys looked cross and made an odd piping sound, but the rest of them nodded.

The flame-haired man looked at Willow and said, 'You have a courageous heart. It will lead you to foolishness – this we can see. While we cannot encourage you to continue, we know you are unlikely to heed our advice, so we will give you something that might help.'

Willow stared. From the corner of her eye she saw Oswin share a confused look with Essential, muttering something like, **'This better be good, after all the monster-'andling they been doing.'** He glared at the wind monkey who kept trying to pet him.

'We wish to offer you this,' said the horned woman, handing Willow a small bright blue seed in the shape of a tear. 'A seed from the Great Tree itself. It will grow wherever you need it to. We hope, however, that you will have no cause to use it – that you are prevented from your search.'

'**WOT?**' There was a harrumph from within the hairy green bag.

Willow blinked. '**Wot**' indeed. It sounded like the forest-touched community was half giving its blessing and half giving them a curse. She felt something ominous creep inside her heart at their words, underneath her frustration. What terrible danger lay ahead that these creatures were so unwilling to even mention, let alone send her into?

Willow took the seed with a frown. She wasn't sure how a seed would help with anything really.

'You may go now,' said the woman, and several of the creatures pushed them all towards Feathering. One leaf-haired woman picked up Willow and another helped Essential climb on to his back. The hairy carpetbag, minus Oswin, was handed to them by an elf. It all happened so fast Willow didn't get a word in.

'Well, I say!' protested the dragon as several wind monkeys pressed against his hindquarters, encouraging him to take off with his cargo. 'First we're kidnapped, then we're asked to kindly push off?'

'Oi, **enough O'** that,' yelped Oswin as the wind monkey, who was rather enamoured with him, tried to give the kobold a large squeeze round the middle.

'*Nice kitty,*' it whispered, patting his head.

'**Fer the LAST TIME, yew infermerol** *beast,* **I is NOT a cat! I IS THE MONSTER FROM UNDER THE BED!**' growled Oswin, turning bright orange, steam coming off his ears. He shot away from the monkey, skittered on to the dragon's back and dived into the hairy green bag.

'Quite right, Oswin,' roared the dragon. 'No respect! I am not the sort of beast who longs for the "good old days". HOWEVER, if this were a thousand years ago, I wouldn't have given a second's thought to eating you all . . . But I am a beast of honour, even if you creatures are not.' Smoke curled from his nostrils, and he hissed in his windy voice, 'THOUGH, if you prod me one more time, monkey, I may just CHANGE MY MIND.'

The wind monkey seemed to swallow and stepped back, making a low trilling sound, as the dragon launched himself into the air. Sprig followed close behind.

Feathering picked up speed, clearly wanting to put

as much distance as he could between them and the forest of Wisperia.

'That was just so weird,' said Essential.

Willow nodded. '*So* weird.'

'I had this strange feeling that she wanted to say more – like the flame-haired man was stopping her from speaking,' whispered Essential.

'I thought so too.' Willow shook her head. 'I wish I knew what language they were using.'

There was a mumble from the hairy carpetbag.

'Pardon?' asked Willow.

She could see Oswin's eye looking at her through the hole in the bag. **'Lurole.'**

'Loo roll?' said Essential with a giggle.

There was the tinkly sound of laughter from the dragon. '*Liral*,' he corrected, snorting. 'The first language – the oldest in Starfell.'

Willow gasped. It was centuries old. It was said that the people who had spoken it had all died out long ago.

'The forest is as old as Starfell itself. Magic came there to hide after the Long War, when it was almost stamped out by the Brothers of Wol. Wisperia has kept many secrets. Perhaps it is not so surprising

that some of its inhabitants still speak Liral,' said the dragon.

'Did you understand what they said?' asked Willow, leaning towards the dragon's ear.

'Not all – I'm very rusty. When I was young, there were still a few dragons who spoke it when they needed to trade with the old magicians or settle territorial disputes without fire – which back then wasn't often, fire being the top choice,' he admitted with a hollow laugh. 'Old beasts, you know. But I did catch something . . . Something about the darkness, or shadows . . . *Mirali.* I can't quite recall the exact translation, but I think it's "death promise" or something.'

Willow had no idea what that meant, but it didn't sound good.

The dragon's golden eye followed the raven as he sped on ahead, leading them towards the town of Library. 'He might know, though.'

Willow frowned. 'Sprig?'

'It looked like he understood them, the way he was listening. Didn't you think it was strange how he never said a word?' asked Feathering.

Willow shared a look with Essential. 'I don't think

so, Feathering. If he knew, he would tell us. He's only trying to help. Besides, he can't speak when he's in raven form. He said that the magic doesn't affect him as much when he's transformed, so maybe that's why he stayed as a bird.'

There was a low grunt from within the carpetbag. It seemed the kobold wasn't so sure.

16

A Town Called Library

They flew for some time, past Wisperia and the floating Cloud Mountains, and over a long winding river. Willow and Essential had managed to strap themselves to Feathering with some strong tree vine that Sprig brought them from the forest, and so they managed a few hours' sleep.

Around lunchtime, they awoke to Feathering's triumphant cry, 'We're here!'

'That must be Library!' Willow said as they neared a town that seemed, from up high, to be made entirely of books.

'Oh NO, *it's even more 'orrible than I remembered*,' whispered Oswin. This was followed by a loud sneeze.

The thing that Willow hadn't quite imagined when considering a town called Library was that it was, in

fact, a collection of enormous buildings, which, instead of being plastered or decorated with tiles or bricks, seemed to be clad with shelves, each one stacked with BOOKS. Some of the buildings, though, were huge glass cubes through which Willow could see rooms with velvet armchairs and bookshelves so high you had to use a ladder to reach the top. It was like a vast, grand estate, covered in books, that sprawled on for miles.

There were flats and terraces and even small courtyard gardens, where people were reading or whispering, bent over books. In the centre of town, there was a giant glass dome, where one could view the night sky, and beside this was a giant clock – shaped like a book, of course – which struck one as they flew over it.

As they descended, they saw that many of the people who lived in the enormous bookish town were hurrying to and fro, some wearing long periwinkle-blue robes. Everywhere Willow looked was a riot of colour and paper and magic. It smelt of dust, memory and something that felt like promise.

She and her friends landed in a small field not far away, in a patch of long silver grass that blew back from the force as Feathering found purchase.

Sprig flew down and changed back into a boy for the first time since their capture by the forest people.

'Have you been here before?' Willow asked him as they headed towards the town. The paths in Library were wide – wide enough even for a dragon.

'Once, long ago,' he said.

She nodded. 'Are they all librarians here?'

'Yes, everyone who's born here. It's one of the

biggest magical settlements in Starfell.'

'Really?' she said in surprise. He nodded.

Feathering looked around. 'That's a lot of books. What happens when it rains?'

'There's some sort of protection on the books, so they don't really get wet. Some kind of old magic,' Sprig explained.

'Wow. Can anyone take a book?' Willow asked in awe. At home, there was really just the one bookcase, and she'd read all of those books twice. There was the travelling library, of course, but it was a bit sad as far as libraries were concerned. It only came to Grinfog after it had already been to the big towns of Grinlemmon and Lael, and it always seemed to have the same pile of books – the ones nobody wanted – for her to choose from.

'Yes,' replied Sprig, 'though you do have to leave a little card and use the special code they assign you.'

Essential was surprised. 'Even when everyone here is a librarian?'

From within the hairy bag there was snort. **'Especiallys COS they're all lib-brains.'**

When Willow had thought of a place called Library,

she'd imagined that it would be very quiet, and that the people would be timid, but this didn't seem to be the case. There was a lot of running and laughter. Boys and girls went by on broomsticks, racing about, their bags full to bursting with books.

In fact, two young girls riding tandem on a rather long broomstick with twin seats flew overhead, and they heard the red-haired one say, 'Oh, it's a *cloud dragon* – see the distinctive feathers, as opposed to scales? Blue, which means it's likely to be male, though green or red has been known. Thought to be extinct, but has been spotted with offspring as near as Grinfog, of all places, recently.'

The other girl nodded. 'I read that paper too. Ferocity level?'

'Low, unless provoked, then rather high. Well, if Marlespoon's early diaries are to be trusted,' said the redhead.

Her friend nodded again. 'Best to cross-reference with the works of Sybil the Sensible?'

'I agree. Shall we?'

Nodding, they flew on.

'Well, I say,' said Feathering, rather taken aback. 'They could just have *asked* me!'

Willow looked at Essential and the two stifled a giggle.

Sprig nodded. 'You'd think that, but then you aren't a book, so it's doubtful they would trust your word.'

Feathering snorted at that.

'I'm surprised that they didn't scream when they saw Feathering,' said Willow. 'I mean, when we went to the Midnight Market, it was pandemonium, remember?'

Feathering nodded. He looked like he might have preferred that in retrospect. 'Respectful,' he said with a tinkly sort of laugh.

Willow and Essential shared another grin.

'Nothing surprises them here – they've read it all. See those ones?' said Sprig, pointing to a group of men and women who were wearing the long blue robes Willow had spotted earlier. 'They're the Secret Keepers.'

'Secret Keepers?' said Willow in surprise. 'Are they different to the other librarians?'

'Well, some say they're the rebels,' came a voice from behind. 'The ones who go against the grain, who have dangerous ideas about things like *commas* . . .

and where we should really stick 'em!'

Willow turned. Behind them stood a youngish woman, dressed in a periwinkle-blue robe that skimmed the ground. She had very long pale hair and enormous, twinkly brown eyes. There was something of a smile about her lips. She laughed. 'I almost got thrown out for my ideas about that at the last council meeting actually.'

Willow couldn't help liking her immediately. 'You're one of them,' she guessed. 'A Secret Keeper?'

'Yes. Pleased to meet you,' said the woman. She held out a rather ink-stained hand, then tried to rub the ink away – but only made it worse by spreading it to her other hand too. 'Sorry,' she said, 'been scribing all morning. I am Copernica Darling, Secret Keeper and part-time Library guide.'

'I'm Willow, and this is Feathering, Essential and Os—'

'**Shhh,**' said a voice from the bag. '**I told yew, no.**'

Willow cleared her throat and introduced Sprig instead.

'Pleased to meet you,' said Copernica. 'I've never met a cloud dragon before . . . or any other kind of dragon to be honest.'

'There aren't that many of us left really. I was the last of my kind for half a millennium till I met my mate, Thundera. We keep to ourselves mostly,' said Feathering.

'Oh,' said Copernica, blinking. 'Right, well, if that's the case, all I can say is they have a bit of a funny habit of –' she cleared her throat – 'sort of keeping unusual creatures for observation around here . . . you know, if they manage to catch them. It's one of those things we have conflicting ideas about. Personally, I don't think it's a good idea to make powerful creatures *violently mad*. But I was outvoted on that. Again. So, just a friendly warning . . .' She laughed awkwardly. 'Maybe stay away from the section near the back there, where the library wizards congregate.' She pointed up ahead, then turned her dark eyes back to Feathering and said warmly, 'Not that I think they'd be able to hold you, of course – without a fight anyway.'

'I should hope not,' said Feathering, who seemed to approve of her respectful comments.

From within the bag there was a low harrumph. **'They tried to documents me as the last kobold! I could 'ave fought 'em off too . . . 'Tis not my fault they put this stuff on me so I couldn't EXPLODE, else I would 'ave . . . Carbuncled lib-brains. Staying 'ere 'ad nuffink ter do wiff the cake . . .'**

'Cake?' whispered Essential.

'*Nuffink* ter do wiff it,' repeated Oswin.

Willow was beginning to suspect it had *everything* to do with it. Cake usually did with Oswin.

Copernica stared at the bag with wide eyes, then opened her mouth.

Willow raised a hand and whispered, 'Don't ask.'

'O-*kay*,' said the Secret Keeper. 'Um, well, anyway – as I mentioned, I'm a bit of a guide to Library. Well, on Wednesdays and Fridays. As Secret Keepers, though, it's our job to uncover the magical history of Starfell, particularly the lost or hidden accounts. We spend a lot of time peering under people's floorboards or digging up artefacts.'

198

'Really?' said Willow with some surprise. She'd thought most librarians just filed books on to shelves. 'And then you bring them here?'

'Yes. I'd say we have the largest collection of magical history in all of Starfell, and it's not all books. There are some practical elements too – where we put what we've learnt into use. Tools, instruments – all the kinds of things that help keep all of this together, you see.'

'Wow,' said Willow. She reached into her pocket for the StoryPass and asked, 'Like this?' It was currently pointing to '*Cup of Tea*?' which Willow always thought was one of its sillier suggestions – though, to be fair, she would have liked nothing better right then . . .

The young woman frowned as she peered at the StoryPass. She tested the weight of it in her palm, then flicked it with a fingernail. 'Amazing! I've only seen one of these early models of the Fable Chronologica before! These were rather good – could be used for more than just cataloguing.'

She beamed as the needle swung round and pointed to '*There be Dragons*'. She looked up at Feathering. 'Ah, precisely. It's a good model – the later ones are rather pedestrian. I'm afraid we lost that battle with the Grand Council, among others.' She sighed and handed the StoryPass back to Willow with a wink. 'Keep that one safe. They do tend to get bothersome here about these old models and attempt to recall them.'

'Actually, perhaps you could help us,' said Willow. 'It's magical history that we're here for really. About plants.'

'Ah,' said Copernica. 'What sort of plants?'

'Magical ones. Ones that have been linked with the art of forgotten telling.'

'Oh?' said the Secret Keeper. 'Most interesting. That'll be in the Old Library Gardens! Come with me.'

17

The Old Library Gardens

The Old Library Gardens were deep in the heart of Library. To get there they went along dusty, book-lined corridors, up and down draughty staircases and past glass cubes, inside which people were sitting next to roaring fires on plush velvet sofas.

'But it's so warm outside,' noted Willow, looking at them in surprise.

'Not in some of these homes. Most people in these parts like to set the weather themselves,' said Copernica, showing Willow a large stone weather dial in the shape of a sun outside a block of flats. It had several points, such as **'DEEPLY UNPLEASANT, INFERNAL SUNSHINE'**, *'HEAVY SNOW, SLIGHTLY FROSTBITTEN'*, *'Rainstorms and hot chocolate'* and, lastly, *'Sleepy cat on warm windowsill'*.

'Oh, these are interesting,' said Willow, wondering

which she'd most prefer. Possibly anything with chocolate, she mused.

'I won't get into the whole theory behind each, but it does depend on the sort of book you're reading,' said Copernica, eyes twinkling.

While Willow wondered about this, and which book was likely to merit, say, '**DEEPLY UNPLEASANT, INFERNAL SUNSHINE**', they walked on towards the gardens. Willow was surprised to find that even in the heart of the old town the streets and corridors were still wide enough for Feathering, so she asked about it.

'Well, interestingly, the town's founder, Jellop the Obscure, actually had a dragon,' said Copernica.

'HAD a dragon?' growled Feathering softly.

Copernica's eyes bulged. 'I mean, um, had a dragon *friend*.'

'Ah yes. For a moment there I thought you were implying he was a *pet*,' said Feathering.

Copernica seemed to realise this at the same moment she remembered that she was stuck inside a corridor with a rather large dragon. 'Er, not at all!' she said brightly, eyes wide. 'Well, mustn't dawdle – this way to the gardens.' And they raced past building

after building, the tour suddenly cut short.

Willow heard a quiet chuckle from the dragon.

The Old Library Gardens were a collection of mazes, the neatly pruned hedges acting as shelves filled with thousands of old books about plants and magic. Dotted around the enormous hedges were vast magical topiaries that seemed to change shape as Willow stared at them. There were some that looked like children sitting on the lawns, until one shifted to change into a dragon, and another into what looked like a cat.

'They're incredible,' breathed Willow, thinking that Nolin Sometimes would *love* them.

'Mischievous,' said Copernica.

'Really?'

'No, that's their name. They're part of the Mischievous genus, known as the mischief topiary. They enjoy playing tricks . . . Not many people visit these Old Library Gardens. Well, there's not much call for magical botany unless you have the skill, and very few do, as you may know. And with so few visitors it's understandable that they're putting on a bit of a show,' sighed Copernica as one turned into a child again and stole the glasses off Essential's nose.

Essential shot after it, coaxing, 'Give them back, c'mon . . . There's a good, um, *plant.*'

There was a snigger from the carpetbag. This stopped immediately when the cat-shaped shrub started to paw at it and it began to smoke slightly. **'Oh *nooo,* oh, *me greedy aunt, stop* that!'**

'I am a dragon . . . who breathes *fire,*' warned Feathering as a gang of the topiary children tried to

climb on his back, one pulling at his ear. At this, they suddenly sprang back to their usual positions, each one looking just a little forlorn.

Willow shot the dragon *a look*.

'Apologies, young Willow. I don't enjoy playing the beast, but we do need to get a move on,' said Feathering. 'And this looks like it might take us forever,' he added, his golden eye taking in row upon row of maze shelves.

This was, alas, very true.

'You can ask it for what you want,' said Copernica.

'What do you mean?' asked Willow.

'Well, for instance, if I wanted to know about the genus and other properties of an old magical plant, like, say . . .' She fished around for an example.

Willow suggested the first thing that popped into her mind. 'Grumbling Gertrudes?' Though the purple fruits always reminded her of Granny Flossy, which made her chin wobble for a moment, and suddenly there was a strange popping sound.

From within the hairy bag she heard Oswin moan, **'Where'd the lining go?'**

Willow blinked. Had she made that disappear?

No one seemed to notice her distress. Copernica, it seemed, had decided not to mention the noises she kept hearing from Willow's bag. Perhaps when you were a Secret Keeper you were trained to turn a blind eye to things like that.

'Okay. Come with me,' she said, and they followed her to a clearing in the middle of the Old Library Gardens where they found what looked like a large brass clock on a waist-high podium. Instead of the time, though, it showed various sections of the library, and it only had one hand. In the centre, inked in fancy lettering, it said: *Information*.

Copernica tapped the glass with her fingernail and said, '*Grumbling Gertrudes.*'

The clock started to whirl round, then paused. The ink that had said *Information* before dissolved and formed the words *Peddling Palatable Potions, Chapter Nine, Trade Secrets, by Festival Moss*, and the clock hand pointed to shelf eleven.

'Moss!' exclaimed Willow. 'That's interesting – that's the same surname as me.'

'Well, magical abilities do run in families. Did anyone in yours have the ability to make potions?' asked Copernica.

Willow swallowed. 'Yes,' she said as sadness filled her chest. She pushed it back down. She didn't have time for that now. 'But what do we do if we don't know what we're looking for?'

Copernica frowned. 'What do you mean?'

'Well, we're looking for the name of a plant we've seen. We don't know much about it, though, except that it belonged to a forgotten teller.'

'Hmmm,' said Copernica. 'Sometimes you can describe it to the dial and it sort of cross-references

things. Otherwise, I'm afraid you might have to look at all of these.' She waved a hand to indicate all the shelves filled with books on magical botany. 'What does it look like, the plant?'

Willow opened the hairy green carpetbag and fished out the jam jar with the small purple iris inside, which then began to shift and swirl into smoke. 'Like this,' she said, showing it to her.

Copernica looked at the jam jar for a moment, then handed it back to Willow. She cleared her throat, then tapped the glass on the library dial and said, 'Magical irises, purple, smoke-like properties?'

The dial whirled round and round, then the clock hand kept moving back and forth between shelves twenty-three and twenty-four.

There were two loud clock chimes, signifying the hour, and Copernica jumped. 'Oh, Great Starfell, I'm late for my meeting with the council – I completely forgot about it. I was so enjoying meeting all of you!'

'Us too!' said Essential.

Copernica beamed. 'What a pity. Next time you're in Library, please do come and visit – I make a really good carrot cake!'

'We'd love that! Thank you so much for all your

help!' said Willow, who had really enjoyed meeting the Secret Keeper and her tour of Library.

Oswin was the only one who didn't seem all that impressed. '**Carrots is not CAKE,**' he muttered from the bag. '**Lib-brains.**'

There were hundreds of books to choose from on shelves twenty-three and twenty-four.

Willow sighed. 'Well, we'd better get started then,' she said, opening a book that spoke of purple irises that were used in blood curses. 'Gosh, this is a bit dodgy,' she added, scanning it. The pictures, however, weren't like the plant in her jar. She stared at it. The petals shimmered, then shuddered.

'This one isn't especially helpful either,' said Sprig, showing them one that spoke about using irises in a garden border to protect against magical pests.

'Or these,' said Essential, who was paging through a historical book that described the changing climate of Starfell and how it affected the plants.

Then Essential spotted a thin blue book that looked handwritten. She picked it up and gasped. '*The Lost Art of Forgotten Telling: A Year in the Garden.*' she breathed, 'by Nolin Sometimes!'

They all shared a look.

'This must have it!' breathed Willow, sitting forward excitedly.

They paged through it. There were hundreds of detailed botanical drawings, including the magical memory flower and the bliss flower. There was also the rather creepy carvery, which she'd seen in a jar just the night before.

On the page next to each botanical print was a small history of the plant's origins, properties and how it helped in the art of forgotten telling. The text outlined each plant's propagation history, along with the observations of past oubliers.

Willow started going through the pages with more speed, until she caught sight of a purple plant and gasped.

There it was – a simple plant that looked like a purple iris with long, thin, dark blue roots suspended in the air. There were two drawings, one of the plant in its natural state and another of what looked like a house made of purple-and-blue glittery smoke. She read the text aloud.

'Mimic plant. While referred to in the singular form, the plant is a set – a pair of twins that can be planted in different locations. When the iris-like flower has been watered, the plant forms a smoke-like substance and mimics its surroundings.'

Willow gasped. 'I did that! I watered it and then it turned smoky and strange – and turned into . . . well . . . me! It was mimicking me. This must be the mimic plant!'

'That's incredible,' breathed Essential.

'What else does it say? How will it help us?' cried Feathering, and Willow read the rest aloud.

'However, if one dies, the other will not live. It is believed that they can communicate their locations to one another if they are separated. These effects were discovered when the plants were potted in separate locations by renowned oublier, Ready Sometimes. When she submerged the roots of one plant in water at midnight (midnight and the moon having transformative effects on many magical plants), it transformed not into a smoke-like shadow of herself, but displayed instead a replica of the garden where its twin was planted. The plants were used as a means of communicating the secret locations of magicians during the Long War as a way to keep families safe, but this has long gone out of common usage now. See page 73 for more plants that were used during the war . . .'

Willow touched the jam jar plant, but it didn't transform into the smoky substance. 'It needs to be watered! Then it'll change into me again.'

There was a fountain nearby and Essential dashed to get the plant some water. They watched as the smoke seemed to judder slightly in the glass jar, then it transformed into a girl with very curly hair and large glasses, her face beaming. 'If this is part of a pair, then—'

'He must have the other plant!' cried Willow.

'They are used to tell the location of one another,' breathed Feathering. 'Remarkable.'

'Does that mean he can see us now?' exclaimed Essential, pushing up her glasses.

'No,' said Sprig. He leant forward to reread the passage aloud. 'When she submerged the roots of one plant in water at midnight . . . it . . . displayed . . . a replica of the garden where its twin was planted.'

'We have to wait till midnight to submerge the roots. Then we'll know where he is!' said Willow with a wide grin.

Finally!

18

The Ghost Tree

They approached the fountain in the centre of the Old Library Gardens a second time just before midnight.

Though they'd been impatient for night to fall, hope had buoyed them, and they had passed the afternoon strolling along the Library streets. In the evening, they had eaten dinner at a bookish café, which had served Feathering whole baked pumpkins out of one of their windows, to his delight.

As they crept near the fountain now, the topiary children gathered round them at a safe distance from the dragon, curious as to what they were doing. Willow's foot stepped on a paving stone, and it began to glow, like candlelight. Dozens followed as they neared the fountain.

'Wow!' gasped Willow.

'It's like another world at night,' breathed Essential, the lights reflecting in her glasses.

Willow sat beside the fountain and unscrewed the lid of the jam jar. The purple mimic plant glowed slightly under the garden lights. At that moment, the town clock chimed twelve times, and at the final stroke she dipped the jar in the fountain until water submerged the plant's long blue roots.

The others waited as she brought it out of the water and replaced the lid. Nothing seemed to happen at first. The plant turned into glittery purple smoke, forming a miniature version of Willow as she held the jar. Then, very slowly, it began to change into a brighter, electric shade of purple, transforming itself until it resembled an enormous tree surrounded by clouds, with exposed roots that swam in a swirling, smoky blue mist.

Willow brought it up to her eye level and frowned. She recognised it. They all did. 'It's the Great Wisperia Tree.'

'**Yew** means **ter** tell me the other one was **there all this time?**' said Oswin with a groan, an orange paw coming up to cover his eyes. The kobold had dared to venture outside the bag under cover of darkness.

Willow stared. There was even a *tiny house* at the top.

She sighed in despair. Had this all been for nothing?

'It's not Wisperia,' said Feathering. The iris in his golden eye whirred as he stared, but he wasn't focusing on the jar. '*Look.*'

Willow turned from him to the topiary children. They were pointing and seemed scared, their leaves rustling as they trembled. A small one was hiding behind its taller friend. As Willow frowned, they shifted, merging to form the tree, except they did it upside down, so that the roots were exposed to the air, long and enormous. Dotted among these roots were strange figures, whose hands reached up into the sky.

What were the mischief topiaries trying to tell them?

Willow frowned and looked back at the jar. She upturned it to match the upside-down version of the tree the topiaries were showing her, and peered at the miniature, mist-shrouded roots. As she did so, she gasped. There

among them were tiny, ghostly figures, with hands reaching out from the mist and shadows, like they were desperately trying to reach up towards something . . .

She stared, then swallowed. All at once, Willow understood. She gasped and dropped the mimic plant. Essential raised both hands, freezing the jar in mid-air, and she caught it safely. Willow was too freaked out by what she'd discovered to thank her. 'It can't mea—' she breathed, turning deathly pale.

'What?' asked Essential, turning the jar in her hands and pulling a face as she noticed the little figures crawling between the roots and reaching up towards her. Essential's eyes widened in a mixture of fear and disgust.

Willow looked from Essential to the others and found it hard to say the words.

Feathering gasped. 'That's what *mirali* meant. I couldn't put my talon on just what the forest-touched people were saying in the old language, but that's what it was. *Mirali* means the other side – *the abyss*. The mimic plant is not showing us Wisperia, but the ghostly echo of the Great Wisperia Tree down in Netherfell. The forest people must have meant that it was forbidden for them to send someone alive there – because you will lose your soul. That's why they wouldn't help us, and why they believed it was too late. Nolin Sometimes must have been taken by Umbellifer, or her subjects at least . . . That's why the treetop community was up in arms. It is very irregular for her or her wraiths – her undead followers – to come up here, to Starfell . . .'

Umbellifer, the Queen of the Undead.

She was the stuff of nightmares and myth. It was said that she waited in the Mists to snatch souls away to her queendom below: Netherfell, the waiting room where all souls were judged before they were sent to their final resting place. The unlucky, however – the lost souls – were doomed to be with her forever as her subjects.

Willow thought of what Holloway had said about people who had gone through the Mists. *'They haven't really come back, have they? Just their bodies.'*

Her eyes were bright with fear. 'We have to find the Queen of the Undead if we're to get him back?'

Feathering nodded.

'You can't mean . . .?' she asked.

'Yes, I'm afraid I do,' he whispered. 'We're going to have to cross the Mists . . . and enter Netherfell.'

19

The Mists of Mitlaire

The blood drained from Essential's face. 'Enter Netherfell?'

'**Oh, Wol, no!**' cried Oswin. '**Oh, me greedy aunt, why'd yew curse us kobolds? I don' wanna go find the soul-snatching harpy-hag of the underworld!**'

Willow couldn't help but agree. 'But . . . HOW? Even . . . even if we wanted to, we can't. Not without losing our souls.'

She looked at Sprig, waiting for him to confirm this. The only person they knew who could cross the Mists was him – but, like he'd said, that was because he was partly born there.

'Is there another way?' she asked.

'I can help you,' said Sprig. 'It's complicated – as I told you, I can cross the Mists safely. But I can also

219

extend this protection to those who travel with me. If you're in contact with me in some way, you can pass through – and, more importantly, return – with your soul intact.'

The dragon looked at Sprig, his golden eye turning dark, suspicious. 'This is what I feared when I met you. That you would take her there . . .'

'I know,' said Sprig, 'but if I did she'd be safe with me.'

The dragon snorted. 'So long as you didn't leave.'

Sprig nodded. It was true.

Willow swallowed. That was scary.

Sprig looked at them. 'We have other things to worry about, though. Like how we're all going to get there. I can spread my magic, but we can't all fly on Feathering, not without risking his life.'

'What? Why?' cried Willow.

'The Mists are tricky. They are designed to make the traveller weary, and the bigger the beast the worse the effects will feel and the longer it will take to cross. In the Mists, the smaller you are, the quicker you pass. It could take days for Feathering, and exhaust him to the point that he wouldn't be able to make the journey back.'

'Oh no!' cried Essential.

'How will we manage then?' asked Willow. 'On foot, so long as we form a chain and keep hold of you?'

'I think that would be incredibly risky. You'd all be exhausted too – I mean, you aren't Feathering's size, but you're not as small as me when I'm a raven. Besides, we can't walk across the lake.'

They all shared a worried look. Once you were through the Mists, you reached the Lake of the Undead, the gateway to Netherfell.

Willow blinked. 'So travelling on a large creature won't work. But what if the thing that carries you isn't alive . . . like, say, a boat? Is there a waterway through the Mists?'

'Yes, there's a stream that runs all the way to the lake,' said Sprig. 'I think a boat would work.'

'But Willow, how are we going to find a boat?' asked Essential.

Willow grinned at her, and reached into her pocket. Inside it was the small copper harmonica that Holloway had given her in case she ever needed him. She touched it and said, 'Don't worry – it'll find us. Looks like we're going to have to head towards the river, so that I can call on a wizard-sailor friend I made.' Willow pulled out the harmonica, and it gave a soft little hoot.

They flew towards the Knotweed River on Feathering and set up camp along a dry, sandy bank. There Willow blew on the harmonica that was linked to the *Sudsfarer*.

'It'll take a few hours for him to come through, I imagine,' said Sprig. 'We should get some rest. There's a lot we will have to face. Trust me, you'll need it.'

'That's true,' said Feathering, who curled up along the riverbank. There were already snores from within the hairy green bag.

Willow couldn't sleep, though. She sat and waited, worrying about Sometimes, worrying about the state of her magic, and how she would actually get him back from the fearsome ruler of the underworld.

When dawn arrived, there were dark patches beneath Willow's eyes. She turned in surprise at the sound of a distant foghorn. She was cold and stiff from sitting on the ground, but she stood up fast.

'W-w-whaat's that?' asked Essential, yawning and stretching before she stood up to look.

Willow beamed. 'It's Holloway!'

The *Sudsfarer* was making its way up the river in the dawn light. There was the sound of marsh birds and the sky was a pinky gold that glinted off the copper bath-boat.

'That's a boat?' asked Essential, blinking as she pushed her glasses up on her nose. It was reflected in her large lenses.

'Looks like a washtub!' exclaimed Feathering, darting Willow a surprised look.

Willow grinned. 'Well, I think it was . . . once. Wait till you see the feet – they move!'

'So we're going to the most dangerous place in the world in a bathtub?' Essential asked, snorting.

'Um. Yes,' said Willow, who couldn't stop a nervous giggle from escaping too.

Holloway, who had seen them through his copper spyglass, called out, 'Ahoy there!' And then, dropping anchor near the bank, he lowered a set of steps that they could use to climb aboard. Unavoidably, though, they had to wade through cold water to get there.

'Holloway! Hello!' Willow called, then climbed up, the carpetbag tucked beneath one arm. Holloway reached out to take the bag before pulling her into a large bear hug.

'Hello to you too, lass! Came as soon as we got the call,' he said, tapping the side of the boat with a gloved hand, his sea-green eye shining.

'Thanks!' she said.

Essential and Sprig followed after her, and he greeted them.

'This is Essential Jones,' Willow said. 'And over there is Feathering.'

Holloway, who had been smiling all round, gasped. 'Is that a *dragon*?' Incredibly, he hadn't noticed the large blue shape on the ground till then.

'Cloud dragon,' said Feathering from the bank. 'Pleased to meet you.'

Willow ran a hand through her hair as she explained the situation to Holloway. 'I'm afraid, Holloway, that I need a rather large favour actually.' She explained about the mimic plant, and how they would need to cross the Mists of Mitlaire and travel to Netherfell.

'Great Starfell!' he gasped, turning pale.

'Um, maybe we could use your boat – um, if you could give me a few pointers on how to sail it? You don't have to come . . . but I really do need to rescue my friend. His life depends on it. I'm sorry – it's a huge thing to ask.'

'Ah, lass, *Sudsfarer* will only sail for me. And look – the way I see it, being stuck in a tower for a year was huge. Helping the young witch who broke me out? That's a small price to pay,' he said. Then he paused. 'Well . . . apart from—'

'The fing about losing yer soul,' supplied Oswin with a nod. **'Apparentlies, the boy can helps wiff that.'**

Holloway looked from Oswin to Sprig, who nodded and explained about his ability and why it was important that he was on board as they went through the Mists.

'Er, okay,' said the wizard.

Sprig nodded. 'I'll fly in front of the boat for now. Follow me, and wait for me as we enter the Mists, so I can land on the boat. The metal should help to conduct my magic to a wide area, but I'll need to be on board.'

Feathering waded into the river, then climbed aboard the bath-boat, making it sway wildly.

'Great Starfell,' said Holloway, staggering backwards. The boat seemed to groan slightly under the new weight as the dragon made himself a perch that was half on, half off the side of the boat.

'I didn't realise we'd be taking . . . um . . . you,' said the wizard, looking at the enormous dragon occupying most of the boat.

The dragon looked at Holloway and said, 'My apologies for this frankly *undignified* moment, but unfortunately I have been told that I cannot fly across, and I'd very much like to go to ensure the safety of my friends.' Then he looked down at the boat, which had sunk quite considerably in the water. 'Unless,' he sighed, looking at it doubtfully, 'it won't be able to carry me.'

Holloway, it must be said, was the sort of sailor made of sterner stuff, because all at once he straightened and said, 'Dragon, we'd be delighted to have ya on board.' Then he muttered that a little firepower was not a bad thing, and something about strengthening the joints, as he took off a glove. He closed his eyes and touched the boat. 'Buck up there, *Sudsfarer*! Think strong . . . Think of the stories we'll be able to tell as a dragon barge!' And the boat seemed to rise a little out of the water, the copper gleaming that bit brighter. Willow could even have sworn that it somehow grew a little bigger.

Sprig watched them, then said, 'Follow me.' With

that, he changed into a raven, flew up into the sky and beat his wings as he made his way towards the Mists.

Holloway nodded, taking the wheel. 'You heard him, *Sudsfarer*. All the way to . . .' He hesitated, swallowed and whispered, 'The Mists of Mitlaire.'

And, despite the heavy weight of the dragon on board, the boat began to cut through the water in fast pursuit of the raven's blue-tinged wings.

20

Netherfell

They sailed all day, and it was several hours into the evening when they spotted the Mists.

'Oh no, oh, me aunt Osbertrude, me eyeballs don' works,' breathed Oswin from within the hairy bag.

The Mists were like a living, breathing thing that swirled across their faces in wet, finger-like tendrils, so cold they seemed to cut to the bone.

There was a bump, and Essential screamed, but it was only Sprig landing on top of the weathervane.

The further they went, the denser and thicker the Mists became, the air colder and cloudier. The stumpy bath-boat legs plodded slowly through the shallow stream like an animal wading in mud.

'Steady there, boat, keep going,' called Holloway as the *Sudsfarer* inched forward.

'Doesn't it ever clear?' asked Willow, eyes straining against the endless white horizon.

'No, it gets worse the deeper you go,' whispered Sprig. 'And, after nightfall, they come out.'

'*Oh no, oh, me greedy aunt,*' cried Oswin, and the bag at Willow's feet began to shake.

Willow gulped. *They?*

'Hold the wheel here, lass,' said Holloway. 'I think I might still have a banshee wail down below. That'll get this ol' guy moving pronto.'

'Banshee wail?' asked Essential. 'Aren't they a bit . . . well, illegal?'

The wizard reappeared moments later with a thick brass cylinder clasped firmly between his gloved hands. Whatever was inside seemed to rattle as if it were alive. Holloway fed the canister into a little chute underneath the patchwork sail and replied, 'Frowned upon, more like, but necessary in the right circumstances. See, we sailors have to be creative when it comes to fighting the elements. Sometimes there's just no wind to speak of and ya can find yourself in the deep without a paddle to yer name, if ya know what I mean. Well, anyroad, that's why most of us have got one of these stashed away . . .

229

Ya know, in case of emergencies.'

He gave them a wink. 'Ya might want to clamp yer hands firmly over yer ears, mind,' he added. Then he pushed down hard on the cylinder, sending it speeding down into the chute. It sank for a moment, then whatever was inside shot up like a rocket with a bloodcurdling cry. The moment the sail caught the shriek, it gusted to life and the *Sudsfarer* began to glide so fast they were knocked off their feet, the terrifying scream ringing in their ears. The boat's short, stumpy legs motored away like they were in a race, and even the Mists seemed to let them pass through more easily, clearing a path for them.

'Amazing!' cried Willow, gripping the edge of the boat.

'Oh, me EARS!' wailed Oswin.

As they hurtled through the Mists, the air began to clear a little, and at last the boat entered a lake. The water was black, with almost no reflection, though every now and then they could see something with eyes and hands rising above the surface.

The hairs on the back of Willow's neck stood on end, and she and Essential clutched each other in fright.

'Great Starfell!' breathed Feathering.

Suddenly Oswin's panicked cries reached a deafening crescendo. **'Oh no! OH, ME 'orrid aunt! Oh, 'tis the end I tells yeh, the end!'**

Essential's eyes were huge in her face. 'Is that – a waterfall?'

Willow could also hear a noise in the distance. She paled. With horror, she realised it must be the long, slow drop all the way down to the dark underworld of Netherfell.

They gasped. The boat tried to swim backwards, its little legs doing a frantic kind of doggy paddle, but it was futile – the current, combined with the remaining thrust of the banshee wail, was pulling them down.

'BATTEN DOWN THE HATCHES!' cried Holloway. And, at their blank stares, he hollered, 'Hold tight!'

They did as instructed and all began to scream as the *Sudsfarer* reached the edge, tipped forward . . . and dropped.

Willow's stomach seemed to dive into her chest, and she held on to the hairy carpetbag for dear life. *'AAAAAAAAAAAGHHHHH!'*

They fell for what seemed an eternity and the blink of an eye, all at the same time.

Then, suddenly, the boat hit something with a thud. It swayed dangerously before it righted itself.

Willow and her friends all staggered unsteadily to their feet. Looking around, they found that they had landed in something like water, but not quite as solid – as if it were made not of liquid but of shadow.

'We must be in Netherfell,' breathed Essential.

They all stared in horror and awe.

In the landscape around them there was an absence of colour – or perhaps the faded memory of it. The air was misty and grey and everything around them seemed made of dark smoke or blue shadow.

Willow swallowed as she stared. Up ahead, alongside the shadow river, was a large, creepy forest. It was packed with giant, twisted trees, and dominating it all was an enormous one the size of several farmhouses stacked together, rising high towards smoky, swirling blue fog. It reminded Willow a little of Wisperia, or at least a dark reverse side of Wisperia – an echo or a memory made of shadow.

Instead of real bark and leaves, the forest seemed to have been made from the memory of what the trees once were. Though, at the same time, there was something almost alive about them. *Undead,* Willow realised with a shudder as the boat sailed past a clump of trees that seemed to bend and move. She could see decaying vines that slithered as they passed and smell the scent of rotten leaves.

The boat came to a stop as they neared what looked like a small black beach, and Holloway dropped the copper-kettle anchor. 'We're here,' he whispered. The wizard threw the small set of steps over the side, and Essential, Sprig and Willow climbed down.

'H-how – how will we find her?' asked Willow as they disembarked, looking ahead through the trees.

'I should imagine she will find us,' said Essential, who sounded terrified. 'Or maybe she'll send her undead subjects to bring us to her.'

'Why – why do you say that?' asked Willow with a gulp.

Feathering hefted himself off the boat, which seemed to buoy itself more upright with a groan of relief, but the dragon looked grim. 'Because it looks like they are already on their way.'

Willow gasped, frozen to the spot, as shadowy wraith-like figures raced towards them. As they

neared, Willow's heart thundered in her chest. The creatures resembled monstrous women with long, vine-like hair and stick-like fingers that ended in pale, twisty fingernails. Their eyes were like pinpricks of hollow light.

'*Oh NOOOOOOO,*' whispered Oswin.

Willow's knees trembled as the wraiths reached them and she tried to back away.

'No!' shouted Holloway. He tried to come to their aid, but as he was rushing down from the boat he was dragged back by something large, tentacled and monstrous that emerged from the shadowy river.

Willow watched helplessly as she was grabbed by the wraith-like women.

'Holloway!' she shouted.

But, before she could do anything more, she and the others were being whisked towards the heart of the forest, towards a small clearing filled with shadowy plants, spikes and thistles.

In the centre of the clearing was a throne made of what looked like diamonds and opals. Willow gulped, as there on the throne was the most terrifying yet hauntingly beautiful creature she had ever seen.

She was dressed in a gown made of shadows and the roots of trees, with pale blossoms dotted throughout the long black hair that waved in the air above her head as though she were underwater. Very subtly, the figure shifted before their eyes like black ink. Her face was pale marble with deep, dark eyes that seemed as if they were quietly examining their very souls.

'Welcome,' she said in a voice that sounded like the rain before thunder. 'We've been expecting you.' Then she smiled, which was somehow even more terrifying.

'We?' asked Willow.

Which was when she saw Moreg.

'Willow!' gasped Moreg Vaine as she was dragged forward by a wraith. 'I didn't want you to come here!' She looked at Sprig. 'You were supposed to keep her away.'

Willow looked from Moreg to Umbellifer. What was going on?

The Queen of the Undead stood up. 'Never mind that for now,' she said, conjuring what looked like a tiny bird made from shadows in her palms. It flew at once into Moreg's mouth, and the witch thrashed her head from side to side, unable to speak.

'What have you done to her?' cried Willow, attempting to rush forward. But the wraith at her side held her back.

The queen cocked her head, waving a set of long, thin fingers that looked like birch bark. 'Nothing to worry about – she's safe. She's rather useful to me,' she said, looking at the witch, who was still fighting against her restraints, trying wordlessly to help.

There was a faint **'Oh no,'** from the carpetbag at Willow's feet.

'Come forward, my child,' commanded the queen.

Willow blinked, confused, and took a step forward.

The queen shook her head. 'Not you, girl.'

Willow turned to look in shock as Sprig stepped up. There was a gasp from Essential as a smaller throne appeared next to Umbellifer's.

The queen smiled her ghastly grin. 'You have earned your seat at last, child.'

21

*The Boy Made of Shadow and Feathers

'I knew we shouldn't have trusted you!' Feathering growled. Smoke curled from the dragon's mouth as he made to launch himself at Sprig.

In an instant, the queen spread her hands and a great beast with wide antlers and gleaming red eyes rose up from the shadows. It charged at the dragon, and with a thunderous roar they began to fight.

Willow watched with wide, fearful eyes, then turned to Sprig. Her heart felt like it was tearing apart.

'Sprig – I don't understand. What's going on?' It seemed like the queen was implying that Sprig was working for her, but that *couldn't* be true . . . could it?

He shook his head rapidly at Willow's baffled expression, taking a step back away from the queen. 'Willow – I – I can explain. It's not how it looks . . .' Sprig gazed back up at the queen, his dark eyes

beseeching hers. 'You don't have to do this,' he said. 'It doesn't have to be this way.'

The queen steepled her long fingers. 'But I do. Don't turn back from your path now, child. You did well. You led her right to me.'

Moreg managed somehow to free herself from the wraith holding her, and the queen frowned in annoyance, then curled her fingers so that ropes of ghostly weeds crawled out of the ground and restrained the witch more securely. Moreg began to thrash, her voice still silenced by the shadow bird, but she mouthed a wordless scream for Willow to run.

The queen looked at the witch, her dark eyes glittering. 'Ah, Moreg. She did all she could to prevent you from coming here. Even now she thinks she can change her fate. She's strong, I'll grant you that,' admitted the queen. 'But that is sometimes a weakness, especially when you can't imagine that someone would dare to cross you . . . She thought that Sprig was doing her bidding, diverting you away, using his raven friends to blow you off course so that you wouldn't be able to come. He played his game carefully, slowly, to throw her off the scent – what with her ability to see things before they happen –

but he was working for me all along.'

Willow blinked, then looked up at Sprig, who couldn't meet her eyes. Her heart plummeted to her toes.

'You tricked us?' she gasped. Anger and sadness washed over her, and she felt her fists clench at her side. She'd thought that Sprig had saved her from the Brothers of Wol out of kindness, but he'd only been trying to keep her alive so that he could bring her here to Umbellifer. This whole time, while her friend's life hung in the balance, Sprig had known where he was and let them go on a wild goose chase across Starfell . . . well aware that they would eventually meet the same fate. He must have been laughing at her the entire time.

'I'm sorry,' whispered Sprig. Then, with a pained look in his eye, he changed into a raven and launched into the shadowy sky, vanishing from sight.

Willow saw spots before her eyes as tears misted them, and a bloodcurdling scream lodged itself in the base of her throat at his betrayal. She thought of Essential, of Oswin and Feathering, of Holloway, her friends that she had advised to trust this boy . . . the boy Oswin and Feathering had tried to warn her about from the start. Were they all doomed now, trapped here with no escape, because of her? Anger, shame and pain all clashed together, and Willow was soon finding it hard to breathe.

Amid her panic there was a loud popping sound, followed by a strange silence that should have been filled with the sounds of Oswin's panicked wailing and Feathering's roars.

Willow opened her eyes, only to fall to her knees in horror. Oswin, Feathering and Essential had all disappeared. She'd made her friends *vanish* into thin air.

She felt as if her heart had been torn from her chest.

'*No!*' she screamed.

The only ones that remained were the queen, her wraiths and the helpless figure of Moreg, still bound in vines.

Umbellifer floated above Willow, her hair studded with pale blossoms, shifting and billowing in an imperceptible wind.

She'd moved so fast that Willow hadn't even had a moment to see how she'd done it. All she knew was the terrifying, thunderous sound of her own heartbeat pounding in her ears, and the feeling of being utterly alone. The weight of her grief was heavy and pressing down on her.

'He did well in bringing you here . . . I believe you may be useful for us, in the days and weeks to come, for what we may need to fight. Your magic ability is useful,' said the queen, who seemed pleased. 'Rarely do I keep souls for my own purposes, but there are times when even I must set aside the rules.'

Willow felt the blood rushing into her ears, her fear so thick she could smell the stench of it, like rotten fruit. Her mouth was dry, but somehow, despite a lead weight on her shoulders, she stood up slowly to face Umbellifer. 'Is that why you took Nolin Sometimes? You wanted his power for your own?'

The idea that the queen would come up to Starfell to snatch souls she thought were useful was a horrible thought.

Umbellifer's form shifted and flickered like a candle against the wind. 'That is just an added benefit. I can only commit a breach when the reasons are

compelling enough. The only other way to draw a soul down here is for them to *decide* they should come. Like you did.'

Willow was confused. 'So why did you take him then, if it wasn't to steal his magic?'

The queen's face was inches from hers as she said, 'Because I needed to know what he saw.'

Umbellifer flicked a wrist and a swirl of mist coiled round them both. Willow hardly had time to gasp in shock as it carried them to the top of what looked like the Great Wisperia Tree in an instant. When the mist dispersed, Willow found herself in an echo of Nolin Sometimes's moon garden. All the colours were gone, all the life sucked out. It was filled with concentric circles made of shadows.

'This world is a mirror,' Umbellifer explained, 'of the one above. What has gone on before trickles down here eventually, through the souls of those who have departed – whether human, animal or plant. I have been listening to these memories, paying attention to the signs . . . just like your witch,' she said, with what looked almost like a smile. 'I have seen that something is coming . . . something to threaten us all. I needed to know more. And then I found this.'

The queen circled a finger, and Willow noticed a wraith-like memory flower by their feet. It looked like a ghostly version of the very flower Willow had once seen in Sometimes's moon garden. He had taught her how this rare and special plant could reveal a secret under the light of the moon before it died. They had asked it who had taken the missing Tuesday, and it had answered them.

'The memory flower told of the boy who took away the day – *the boy called Silas cast the spell hidden within the fortress.* I knew this was linked to the signs that something terrible was coming, but I needed to discover more. I needed to find the person who knew to ask it this question – which is why I took the forgotten teller.'

The spent petals began to blow apart in the windless air. And there, across the garden, where the scattered remnants of the flower settled, lay a figure with white hair and unseeing pale eyes.

'Sometimes!' Willow cried, and she raced towards him. She knelt beside her friend, trying to wake him. His eyes remained open yet all white. Willow shook him, but he would not wake. His body hung limp in her arms.

The ghostly queen approached Sometimes and touched his shoulder. Her eyes suddenly rolled back in their sockets, turning pale and white like his. Then she let go of him and blinked, and her eyes returned to their usual black. They seemed to gleam as she drifted in the air above Willow. 'I have read his memories, read all that he has seen in Starfell – even things that he missed.'

Sometimes remained lifeless on the ground. 'What's happened to him?' Willow asked.

'He's asleep,' said the ghostly queen, 'or rather he's adrift somewhere between life and death. It's a valuable skill I put to use when I need to read someone's secrets or borrow their magic. It's better if they're not awake.'

Willow felt tears prick her eyes. 'This is someone's life, not some game! Let him go. He would have told you anything you wanted – you didn't need to abduct him. You didn't need to play these cruel tricks on us.'

Umbellifer stared at her. 'You are naive, child. I am not some monstrous ruler seeking only power. He is *needed more here* so that I may prevent what has happened before.'

Willow frowned. 'Prevent what?'

'What do you think? Another war, child.'

22

The Forgotten Tale

Willow stared. 'A war?'

The queen nodded. 'One is coming, of that I have no doubt . . . The signs show that history is set to repeat itself. As I said, most memories trickle down here eventually, but some take millennia . . . and there was a key event that even I, with access to all of this,' she said, indicating the ghostly world at her feet, '. . . missed.'

'What?' asked Willow.

The queen moved fast, her eerie face inches from Willow's as she floated above her. Umbellifer's shape shifted like ink in water, the pale white blossoms in her hair shining, her dark, tunnel-like eyes seeming to peer into Willow's very soul. 'Tell me, child, what do you know of the Long War?'

Willow frowned. It was the worst war in Starfell's history, one that had almost *ended all magic*. 'It began

a thousand years ago. The Brothers of Wol tried to convince the world that magic was unnatural – that it wasn't a gift from the god Wol, but something evil, something that needed to be destroyed. This led to a war, and many magicians died . . . and for a long time everyone believed that they had succeeded in stamping out all traces of magic.'

'Go on.'

'But they hadn't, not really . . . because, after many years, magic came back.'

Willow remembered what Granny Flossy had told her, that magic never really dies – it simply waits until we're ready for it. She looked up at the queen, wondering if she should tell her the rest . . . about what she and Moreg and the others had found out in the Brothers of Wol's fortress, Wolkana. Perhaps telling Umbellifer what she knew might help to ensure the release of Sometimes and the others, so Willow continued.

'During the war, the old magicians gathered together their most powerful spells to try and fight the Brothers. Everyone thought those spells had been lost or destroyed, but we found out they'd been hidden in Wolkana for centuries. The High Master of the Brothers of Wol said it was to protect the world from this powerful magic . . . but Silas, the Brother who stole the missing day, said that that was a *lie*. He believed that the real reason the Brothers had kept the spells all those years ago was so they could *use* them. My friends and I managed to get back the day Silas stole, but we think he still has the Lost Spells . . .'

The queen's dark eyes seemed to glitter as she hissed, 'Oh, he has more than that, child.'

Willow swallowed. 'What do you mean?'

'Thanks to your friend Sometimes, I have now seen a very important memory. A memory that the forgotten teller read when he was inside Wolkana with you and the others. Maybe it's best if I show you . . .'

Umbellifer waved her hands, and in the air before them the mist and shadows began to change. They shifted to form a scene in what looked like Wolkana. A short-haired boy in long robes scurried down a long, twisting corridor, glancing behind him furtively as if he were afraid someone was watching . . .

Willow gasped. He might have been made of Umbellifer's shadows, but Willow recognised that distinctive walk, that hair. It was *Silas*.

In the shadowy scene before her, he got to the end of the corridor and took out a key from his robes. He looked over his shoulder once again, then opened the door and rushed inside a small room. He seemed to know exactly what he was looking for as he knelt down and lifted a loose floorboard, bringing from under it a small, heavy-looking chest. He opened it and took out a thick book.

Behind him there was a noise, and an old man appeared in the doorway. He was stooped over and using a cane. Oddly, even though the figures were depicted in shadow, Willow could hear them speak, the sound somewhat hollow, like an echo, or a noise from behind walls. 'What are you doing in this room, boy? You know it's the private storeroom of the High Master.'

'I'm sorry, sir, yes – he asked me to bring him the wine for the blessing,' said the boy, blocking the floorboard and the chest from view.

The old man bent forward as he stared intently at Silas. Then a coughing fit took hold of him and, when he at last recovered, he seemed to think better of pursuing the matter. He made a dismissive sound and said, 'Well, hurry up. It's most irregular for him to send someone down here.'

The boy nodded and picked up a bottle from a table. When the old man's back was turned, Silas slipped the book inside his robes.

'Out with you, come on,' said the old man, and Silas followed.

The shadows whirled and the scene changed. Silas was now sitting on a bed in a small cell. He touched the cover of the book. As much as he tried, though, he could not open it. It was tightly shut, as if it had been locked by magic. On the front Willow could see a title

that read **The Testaments of Wol.**

She watched as Silas tried to prise it open with a knife. He then tried to steam it open, perhaps thinking it was glued shut. When this failed, he seemed to think for a long time, and then Willow gasped as he took a penknife from his robes and slit his palm. He touched the title with his blood, waiting expectantly. The book seemed to glow red for a moment, shimmering in an almost violent haze, and then, at last, it opened. On the first page it said, *The private journal of Wollace Humperdink, the Greatest Sorcerer of Starfell.*

And suddenly the shadows faded, and once again Willow saw nothing before her but the echo of Nolin Sometimes's moon garden.

Willow blinked. 'That really happened?' she asked. She felt creeped out by the blood, which, unlike the rest of the shadows, had glowed oddly red.

The queen nodded. 'Yes. Silas read the thousand-year-old journal of the so-called "god", Wol, who was in fact nothing more than a magician named Wollace Humperdink who reinvented himself after the world believed he was destroyed by the elths. He fooled many men and gathered them as his followers – the

Brothers of Wol – and they spread word that magic was unnatural and evil, promising to cleanse the world of it. But Wol's secret plan was to keep all of that magic for himself, so he could become the sole sorcerer of Starfell.'

Willow felt uneasy. In Wolkana, when Silas had claimed that the Brothers had been lied to for years, and that the true goal of the war had been to hoard the magic for themselves, she hadn't known whether to believe him. She certainly hadn't realised that Wol had never been a god at all. She'd heard of that old magician, Wollace Humperdink, but she'd never put the two together before.

The queen went on. 'The Brothers failed to completely eradicate magic a thousand years ago. That we all know. But this memory reveals something catastrophic – that Wol recorded the tale of *how* he stole the magic of Starfell, so that if he could not complete his mission, one day a worthy successor might finish the task.'

Willow panicked. 'But – but if that's true Sometimes would've said something! He would have warned everyone after he had this vision!'

The queen shook her head. 'He didn't understand

the relevance of the memory. Wol didn't spell it out in plain language – he was more careful than that. But I pieced this memory together with the other clues I've gathered from my sources, and I learnt the truth. Even now, as we speak, Silas seeks vengeance for his thwarted plans, and this time he intends to go to extremes to ensure that he is never defeated again!'

Willow felt as if she'd been doused in ice. 'What is he going to do?'

'Don't you understand, child? He is uncovering Wol's method – a terrible ritual that will allow him to rip out all the magic from Starfell! If he succeeds, he will take every last thread of magic from every witch and wizard, every elf and elth, every enchanted creature and plant, from the forest of Wisperia, and my queendom of souls. It will ALL be HIS.'

Willow gasped, horrified, as she tried to imagine her family, and every magical person or creature she knew, drained of their magic . . .

'Unless I act now!' cried Umbellifer. 'Do you see now how I might need a man who can read the past – by reading the memories of everyone he comes across – and a woman who sees the future? Don't you see what assets they will be in fighting this new

257

war? With these skills, I will be able to work out the enemy's weaknesses, identify traitors and predict their next moves! And you, child – you are more powerful than you realise. Your magic is growing. You have already thwarted Silas once, and I believe I can use your powers to fight him again.'

'Y-you're wrong – my powers are broken! They don't work,' protested Willow. 'There must be another way to prevent the war – you don't need to keep us here!'

The queen shook her head. 'This is the only way.'

With that, Umbellifer commanded the shadowy mists again, and they swirled round all three of them, whisking Willow, Sometimes's prone body and the queen back to the forest floor below.

When they landed, Willow barely had time to steady herself before the queen snapped her fingers, and a shadowy figure brought Moreg forward and laid her down next to Sometimes. Her body too had grown still, like his, and her eyes were white.

'No!' shouted Willow, who felt as if her heart had been plunged in ice at the sight of Moreg paralysed by the queen's magic. 'There has to be another way! They would help you if you asked – we're on the same side!'

The queen seemed to sigh as she floated above Willow. 'Humans don't help – they cause destruction. Their emotions, their passions, desires and petty jealousies get in the way. Just look at you. So useful – yet so clouded by your emotions that you can't even see what you have. I need their memories and their abilities – but not their messy human drama. It's not how I like to do things, but needs must. And the time has come for me to add your magic to my collection too.'

Suddenly there was a low, cawing cry. A raven with a smoky blue-black wing appeared above, talons outstretched as it made a dive . . . at the queen.

Sprig attempted to tackle Umbellifer as he landed, transforming into a boy, and he shouted, 'Run, Willow! Quick!'

Willow tried to run, but only got a few steps before thick vines crept across the forest floor and tangled round her feet, holding her tight.

'You dare defy me?' the queen challenged Sprig. 'After everything I have done for you – you who could rule by my side?'

'Yes, because you're wrong! It doesn't have to be this way. I've seen how people can come together. We

could fight as a team,' argued Sprig.

'Like we did the last time, when magic was nearly ripped out of the world?' the queen scoffed. 'You silly boy, you forget where you are. In my queendom, you will play by my rules.' And then she flicked her fingers and vines restrained him, even as he thrashed. In the next moment, Umbellifer's smoke and shadows swirled round him and he was whisked out of sight.

Suddenly it was just Willow and the queen again. Willow sank down helplessly to her knees.

'Look at what all this emotion has cost you. Your friends are here now, lured by their misplaced faith in you,' said the queen. She swirled a hand and a swathe of misty fog appeared, carrying within it the shadowy image of Willow's three missing friends. The mist settled near Moreg and Sometimes, leaving the ghostly impressions of Feathering, Essential and Oswin beside them, looking as if they were sleeping.

Willow gasped. 'But I made them disappear! How are they here . . . with you?'

'Because, though your magic works down here, this is my world, and it must play by my rules. You lost your friends, and *this* is where lost souls end up after all . . .'

Willow felt a sob rise in her throat as she rushed forward towards the lifeless figures of Sometimes and Moreg and the misty image of the others.

Nolin Sometimes was closest. He looked so drained of life. She thought of his love for strange magical plants, his wonderful treehouse home, the way he fainted every few minutes when he was bombarded with memories, how his eyes lit up when he got excited about new discoveries, his loud, barking laugh.

Next she approached Moreg. It was strange to see her face so placid, her usually dark eyes white and devoid of their fire. It was like the thing that made her Moreg was gone . . .

With a heavy heart, Willow turned to the smoky image of her other friends. She stared at the large, motionless figure of Feathering, his pearly feathers seeming dull somehow, and she felt her lip start to shake. She looked from him to Essential, her dear new friend who made her feel like every day could be an adventure. Then her gaze moved to Oswin. Her grief began to cascade over her as she saw the kobold – green now, his fur soft, his beloved crotchety face still and his eyes unseeing – and the tears came at last.

It was old grief, everything she'd pushed down

after losing Granny Flossy, choking and painful. The sorrow was so solid, so enormous, that it blocked out everything else like a wave. Willow could feel the blood rushing in her ears and it was as if the world were escaping her grasp. She began to howl as she slumped to the ground.

She couldn't see for the tears as she cried out their names. It was all her fault! The queen was right – she'd lured them here. She'd chosen to come here, and she'd risked all of them in the process. Everyone who had believed in her had paid such a terrible price. Perhaps her family had been right all along not to believe in her. Look what she'd done!

Willow sobbed into the dark forest and then, somehow, she heard her grandmother's voice from behind her.

'Now, now, lass. Dry yer eyes. Tell me, what is it?'

Willow gasped and looked around. But she couldn't see her. There was just a faint lime-green glow surrounding Willow, like a coronet round her knees. She felt warmed by it somehow, as if it were a small, glowing flame. She blinked back her tears and whispered, 'Are you here, Granny?' Her heart skipped a beat in fear. 'Are you . . . lost . . .' She looked at the faces of her friends. 'Like them?'

'*No, child. I'm the part that lives forever within you. We all leave a little of our souls behind with the people we loved. 'Tis only now that you're in the world of souls and memories that I'm able to speak with you, lass — through the magic of this place. Tell me what it is you're feeling that's making it all disappear? Making you doubt your abilities, and yourself?*'

Willow's lip trembled. It was there, the thing that she'd been pushing down for weeks, trying not to feel. She closed her eyes and fresh tears poured down her face.

'I feel lost. Lost without you.'

Suddenly it was like a dam burst and Willow sobbed. She didn't know who she was any more. All she felt was alone.

'*I am always with you, lass. Those we love never truly fade away. They live in our hearts and in our memories. They give us strength when we need it most.*' Willow imagined more than felt Granny Flossy's finger run beneath her lashes, wiping away her tears. '*You know what you need to do. You can feel it there. Just believe, child.*'

And then there on the shadowy ground appeared Granny's purple hat with the jaunty green feather, which had gone missing from Willow's attic all those days ago. Willow stared at it incredulously. It was like a crack of light in the darkness.

Willow looked up to see the ghostly queen not very far away, floating in the forest behind her – watching her, waiting . . . perhaps wondering what she would do next.

Willow nodded, then got to her feet and closed her eyes. She drew strength from somewhere deep inside, raised her palm to the sky, and concentrated on finding all that she had lost. It wasn't just things: it was her friends, her courage, her self-belief . . . The girl who found lost things had lost *herself . . . but not any longer.*

There was a torrent from above, and the sound of a million spoons descending from nowhere, hitting the forest floor in a clamorous heap. These were followed by beds, and lost coats.

Suddenly a witch with a copper foot appeared and said, 'Well now, child, took yeh long enough! Looks like me remedy worked after all!'

Willow didn't respond. She just kept her eyes closed.

'*Keep going,*' said her grandmother's voice, and she did.

Feathering came next.

'Young Willow!' he shouted. 'What happened? I was fighting that beast . . .'

Willow allowed herself a small grin, but she kept her eyes closed as she concentrated. Then Oswin appeared, landing in her arms with an orange plop. '**Wot choo go and makes me disappear** likes that **for? That's no way to treat a body!**' he complained as he climbed down to the ground.

Next came Essential, pushing up her glasses with a frown.

Willow kept her eyes closed as she continued her search for Moreg and Nolin Sometimes – for their souls that were drifting between life and death, lost under the queen's powerful grasp. It was hard. The queen did not want to let them go. Willow dropped to her knees. It was like her mind was wading through something thick and viscous; it sapped her energy, and she grew weak as she searched and searched.

'*You can do it,*' said Granny Flossy's voice.

She could feel the traces of Sometimes. The queen was holding on tight, but Willow fought back. Her magic might not be the strongest or the most remarkable, but it was *reliable*, and it would be so again! Because this time she wouldn't forget who she was, or what she could do. She pulled with her mind, as if holding on to a fraying rope for dear life. She felt what seemed like the thread that was Moreg, purple-tinged, and Sometimes, pale blue, and pulled and pulled . . . till finally they were free.

She opened her eyes, and there they *were*.

23

The Ferili Seed

M oreg's and Sometimes's sightless eyes turned back to normal.

'Gadzooks!' exclaimed the forgotten teller. 'Am I pleased to see you!'

In his hands was the other mimic plant, which right then looked just like him, a small shadow of a man in a jar.

'I didn't know if you'd find it!' he cried. 'I hoped you would. I couldn't be too obvious about it in my letter in case they found it and stopped it reaching you.' He gave a dry, barking sort of laugh.

Willow grinned. She'd figured that was the case.

'I'm glad to see you too,' said Moreg. 'I'm sorry I tried to prevent you from coming . . . I saw what was happening with your magic – I got a flash of it – and thought it would be best for me to come and get

him, rather than risk your life. I knew you would get a handle on it, but I wanted you to have that time – not force you into this danger, like I did the last time.'

Willow touched the older witch's hand, moved by her words. 'You didn't force me. But at least I understand now.'

'How very touching,' said the queen, suddenly joining them. 'And I am pleased to see you restored to your full potential,' she added, looking at Willow. 'That will be better for my purposes.'

'Enough of this,' said Moreg. There was a clash of thunder, followed by a flash of lightning.

The queen seemed to smile. 'Oh, I did wonder when the fearsome witch I had heard so much about would actually turn up. So it's a fight you want, is that it?'

Suddenly there were dozens of red-eyed beasts circling them all, along with several white, spectral wolves.

'I am, of course, always an obliging host . . .' And, at that, the monstrous beasts began to advance on them.

Pimpernell rolled up her sleeves, coming to stand next to Moreg, her wood-fire eyes blazing. She waved her opal-topped cane threateningly. 'We're gonna unleash more fire down here than you've ever seen before.'

Essential raised her hands and tried to freeze the shadow beasts. It worked for about half a beat. 'Run!' she cried to Willow and Sometimes.

There was a piercing cry and suddenly Sprig appeared in raven form, a vine still tangled round one of his feet. Despite everything that had happened, Willow found she was relieved to see him – relieved that he had escaped Umbellifer's restraints and made his way back to them.

'Follow me!' he called to Willow as he transformed into a boy and led them into the shadowy woods. 'This way!'

Oswin dashed into the green carpetbag at Willow's feet, and she picked it up as they turned and fled after Sprig.

Nolin Sometimes's eyes went pale as he ran, and he dropped into a dead faint.

Willow skidded to a stop and gasped, 'Oh no!'

But thankfully he wasn't out for long. From his prone state Sometimes's eyes turned from white to blue. He sat up and stared at Willow urgently, gasping, 'They gave you a ferili seed?'

Willow stared at him. 'A what?' She felt that now was not the time for them to be discussing things that

didn't immediately involve screaming and running away from ghostly, red-eyed beasts. In the distance, she could see Feathering attacking one, fire streaming out of his mouth.

'A seed from the Wisperia tree! It's genius of them really.' Then suddenly he sank back down into another faint, his eyes white again.

'Oh, Sometimes!' Willow cried, shaking him. The trouble with Sometimes's ability was that he often didn't realise that he fainted when he was seeing a memory.

Oswin jumped out of the bag and hissed at a wolf that was getting dangerously near.

Thankfully, Sometimes's eyes turned blue again and he frowned as he muttered, '*Merali*, well, yes . . . I also wish I hadn't risked you like this – I had no idea at the time that your magic had gone rogue. I thought you might be able to find me from the safety of Starfell.'

One of the beasts Essential had been trying to fend off unfroze. Snarling and snapping, it made its way quickly after them.

'Sometimes! This is not the time! We have to get out of here!' cried Willow, grabbing him by the arm.

'Maybe put your hands over your ears so you don't faint?'

As he raced beside her, he looked affronted. 'I don't faint!'

Behind them, Willow could hear Feathering attacking one of the beasts, and as she ran she glanced over her shoulder. Moreg was fighting with the queen while Pimpernell protected her flank against a group of advancing wraiths by swinging her opal-topped cane. But there were too many of them for the hedge witch to hold back. Willow gasped as Moreg released a bolt of lightning from her fingers towards the wraiths, illuminating the forest.

Willow could well see why Moreg was called the most powerful witch in all of Starfell ... but she was well matched, as the queen retaliated by stirring forth a massive shadow dragon. **'Oh no,** oh, me 'orrid **aunt,'** cried Oswin, who was carrying the carpetbag in his front paws as he raced away from a smaller beast, his ears starting to smoke.

'NOW is the perfect time!' cried Sometimes. 'The seed is from above, from *Wisperia*. It doesn't work with Umbellifer's magic – it'll work with *ours*. Plant it, quick!'

'**Wot?**' cried Oswin, overhearing Sometimes. '**The forgotten teller is** mental **– now is not the time** for **gardenenening.**'

'Trust me!' shouted Sometimes.

'It's in the bag!' cried Willow.

Oswin groaned. '**Oh, me greedy aunt, a curse upon yeh,**' he hissed as a beast came forward, and he delved a paw into the bag to grab the bright blue seed.

Sprig, who was flying above, gave a blood-curdling cry and dived at the shadow wolf, diverting it away from Oswin.

Sensing Sprig's plan to distract the shadow beasts, Essential cried, 'I'll help!' She lifted her hands to freeze another of the advancing beasts while Oswin, Willow and Sometimes ran towards a clump of shadowy trees and hid out of sight.

'Plant it!' cried Sometimes.

The kobold shot the forgotten teller a hard look, but did as instructed, his ears smoking as he dug up a little of the shadowy earth and patted the seed into place. He looked up at Sometimes and shook his head. **'Nutters, the lot of yeh. After this, if I gets out alive, I fink I'm going on an 'oliday. There's a nice dark drain near the cottage . . .'**

As soon as the seed was planted, a small, pale yellow shoot began to grow very quickly. It sparkled like sunshine in the gloom.

'What is it?' whispered Willow.

'Magic,' said Sometimes.

And it grew into a mighty plant, like a beanstalk with thousands of shoots that

began at once to fight against the
shadows, snuffing them out as the plant
grew and spread through the forest. Its
bright blue shoots reached towards the
shadowy beasts and held them back, while a
massive root wrapped itself round the shadow

dragon fighting with Moreg. In the ruckus, Moreg and Pimpernell were able to get away, and raced towards the others.

'Come on, let's get out of here!' cried Sometimes, and together they began to run away from the forest and towards the shadow river.

As they neared, Willow felt an enormous pang of guilt. The last time she'd seen Holloway he'd been dragged off by a monstrous beast, but, with her own capture and everything else that had happened, she hadn't yet stopped to really consider if he was all right. Her heart sank in her chest, and she silently pleaded that he was okay. She couldn't find one friend only to lose another!

She fished out the brass harmonica and quickly brought it to her lips. Behind her the shadow beasts were advancing. She blew on it, and suddenly a large copper bathtub with stumpy legs came hurtling up the river at breakneck speed. Then, through the swirling mists, she saw a familiar figure on board.

Willow's knees almost gave out in her relief. 'Holloway! You're all right!' she cried, a grin splitting her face.

'Willow, ahoy there, lass! Sorry I couldn't find ya sooner – it took me forever to fight off that tentacled monster! Had to set a banshee wail on it—' He stopped suddenly when he saw what was behind them, and he dropped the steps over the side of the boat at once. 'Board now, quick! Quick as you can,' he said, and they all sped on to the boat.

Moreg turned and, with a twist of her fingers, she released a lightning bolt towards a shadowy beast that Feathering had been fighting off.

The dragon rose up fast and dived on board. 'Thank you,' he breathed, sounding exhausted. 'It kept getting stronger as I breathed fire . . .'

'Don't mention it,' said the witch.

Holloway's sea-green eye widened as it took in Moreg, and he seemed to mouth her name silently, then swallow. His face blanched further when Pimpernell climbed quickly aboard, knocking back a shadow beast with her opal-topped cane, her wood-fire eyes glowing with warmth.

'Well, hello there, wizard! This be a mighty interestin' turn of events, you comin' ter rescue us,' she said. 'Mayhap I should have believed yeh when yeh said yeh wasn't gonna use yer new powers fer bad . . .' She looked almost contrite. 'A witch should admit when she's done wrong . . . so I'm doin' that now . . .'

Holloway blinked. 'Um, thanks.' His cheeks turned pink, and then he jumped into action, taking two banshee-wail canisters and loading them into the chute beneath the sail.

'Cover yer ears!' he commanded, and they did, as bloodcurdling cries split the air. The noise kept even the beasts back and the boat sped fast on its stumpy legs towards the black waterfall.

'How on Great Starfell are we meant to get up that?' cried Sometimes. 'Will the banshee wails do it?'

Even Holloway looked uncertain.

'I could try freezing it?' suggested Essential. 'That might work!'

They nodded – it might.

Essential closed her eyes and concentrated with all her might. Then she raised her hands and tried to freeze the downward tumble of the shadowy waterfall. At first it didn't seem to work, then it sort of flickered a little.

Moreg put her hand on Essential's, and there was something almost like a tiny lightning flash, and the whole waterfall froze, becoming a motionless wall of shadowy water.

The boat steamed ahead, powered by the twin banshee wails. Right before they reached the base of the waterfall, Feathering cried, 'Hold tight!' He heaved himself up and launched all his mighty weight against the stern, causing the boat to rock backwards and point its bow up the waterfall.

'Thank you, dragon!' yelled Holloway as the power of the banshee wails took over once more. 'Perfect first-mate work.' Then he nodded, clung to the wheel and said, 'That's right, *Sudsfarer* – all the way up, past the Mists, to the Knotweed River . . .'

As they climbed up the waterfall, Willow's eyes became heavy. She was tired . . . so tired . . . Her body felt drained of energy.

Before she knew it, she was falling back into Sprig's and Essential's arms, fast asleep.

24

Home

Willow awoke to sunshine and the sound of marsh birds as the *Sudsfarer* glided up the Knotweed River towards home.

All the colours were bright and bold. The water shone and shimmered. The sky was a brilliant blue, and along the riverbanks Willow could see the marsh grass, knotweed, the butterflies and the bees.

'Welcome back,' said Moreg, taking a seat next to her.

Willow had been placed on a mound of cushions on the deck. She sat up, blinking in the afternoon light. Near the stern, she could see Nolin Sometimes leaning against the railing as he chatted to Essential and Oswin, who was looking at the world through the copper spyglass. In the sky above, she could see Feathering keeping pace with the boat.

'We were worried about you,' said the witch.

Willow felt a wave of fatigue wash over her as she tried to sit up.

'Relax, you've used a lot of magic – you need to rest.'

Willow nodded. She looked at the witch and frowned, opening then closing her mouth.

'What is it?' asked Moreg.

'Why didn't you just send me a message to tell me not to come to Netherfell?' Willow asked finally.

'I should have – but I couldn't be sure if you would have listened, knowing that your friend's life was at stake. I thought it best to try and keep you safe. The problem was I couldn't rely on my seeing ability – I can't see what happens in Netherfell, just like Umbellifer can't see what happens in the world above. That's why I was unable to predict what Sprig was going to do – his actions were careful, and the fact we were often in different worlds clouded my vision.'

As if he had been waiting for Willow to wake up so that he could speak to them both, Sprig approached them now. He looked unsure of himself. There were deep shadows beneath his eyes, and he bit his lip.

'I'm so sorry about everything. I didn't want to

betray you,' he said, looking at Moreg. 'I believed Umbellifer when she said it was for the best – that we could prevent a war this way. I knew she was going to use your powers, but I never thought she would try to keep anyone in Netherfell for good.'

The witch frowned. She didn't seem angry, just disappointed perhaps. 'You of all people should have known better. She's not someone who plays fairly,' she said. 'But there was something else that was motivating you, wasn't there?'

Sprig looked down at the floor of the boat. 'Yes,' he admitted.

Willow thought of the small throne that had appeared next to the queen's. 'You wanted to rule with her?'

He shook his head. 'Not exactly rule, no. I just wanted to belong. I've always felt a little lost, with one foot in both worlds. Out here, in this world, there have been many who were afraid of me, my powers . . . the scent of death. Umbellifer made me a promise that I would find where I belonged.'

He looked at Willow and gave her a small, shy smile. 'I did find where I belonged . . . but it wasn't down there. I hope we can be friends, Willow.'

Willow felt tears prick her eyes. She nodded. 'I'd like that very much.'

'Very well, boy,' said the witch. 'It was a foolish thing you did, but I can understand why. However, if you cross me again, you will regret it. Leave us for now.'

Sprig swallowed, nodding, then turned to join Essential and Sometimes.

The witch looked at Willow and seemed almost to

grin. 'It's always useful to send a gentle reminder that a witch is not someone to cross . . . Remember that,' she said, tapping her nose, and Willow couldn't help the small chuckle that escaped her lips.

Moreg continued. 'Speaking of witches, we dropped Pimpernell off a little while ago. I've had a chat with her, told her that she needs to make some changes, get an assistant – speak to other witches. She means well, I suppose; she just goes about things the wrong way. I think seeing that Holloway had been telling the truth, that he wasn't going to use his new ability for evil, also opened her eyes. She wouldn't go so far as to admit guilt for locking up someone for a year – not when she believed she was in the right – but I think she can see that maybe she was getting too extreme. The Enchancil will start to look in on her more. It's not good for anyone to have nobody to answer to – like Umbellifer in her own way.' The witch touched Willow's shoulder. 'I should have known one thing, though – that should have been obvious.'

'What's that?'

'That if anyone could save us, it would be you.'

Willow didn't know what to say to that. She felt a blush rise to the roots of her hair. She looked up at the witch. 'I don't know about that. Um, actually, about my magic – how my grief made things disappear – do you think that could happen again?'

Moreg frowned. 'I don't think it was grief that was making it happen.'

Willow stared and the witch explained.

'I think the grief was *preventing* you from using your usual ability. But I have a feeling that something else happened when we were in Wolkana. When you got the spell scroll from Silas, it shouldn't have worked because he'd used a protective spell.'

Willow blinked. 'Why did it then?'

'Because magic wanted you to succeed,' said Moreg.

'What?' breathed Willow. 'I don't understand.'

'The magic of Starfell,' she said. 'It knew what was happening. Maybe it even knew what was coming, based on what had gone before, when it was almost ripped out of the world. Perhaps it sensed that you were trying to help. So it took a chance, and decided to break its own rules. It decided to trust you.'

'It trusted me?'

'Yes, and magic like that always leaves a trace. It touched you and gave you something in return – the other side of your ability perhaps. So you can now

make things appear *and* disappear. Very useful, once you learn how to control it.'

Willow blinked in amazement.

'It also makes you dangerous, which is something you need to be careful about. The Brothers of Wol have been hatching their plans to seize witches and wizards, and Silas is out to steal magic from the world for himself. We will need to be ready.'

Willow nodded. They would.

25

Moss Cottage

A while later, they heard Feathering's trumpeting cry as he signalled his farewell.

'Must get back to baby Floss – he'll be wondering where I am. Come and have some pepper tea with me soon, friends. I'll try to convince the plant to come back . . .'

They waved him off, Nolin Sometimes laughing his loud, barking laugh. 'Good luck with that.'

Holloway moored the boat in a small stream that ran close to Willow's village, then gave her a hug.

Willow reached inside her bag for the copper harmonica to return it to the old wizard, thanking him for all he'd done.

'Keep it, young Willow. That way I know ya can always use it when ya need me.'

She gave him a last hug. 'I will,' she promised.

Willow said goodbye to Sometimes, Sprig and Essential, already making plans for when they would next meet, and then she and Moreg got on their brooms and made their way to Willow's cottage.

There was pandemonium when she arrived.

'Willow!' cried her father, standing up so fast he upended his chair. He looked tired and worried, and Willow couldn't help the stab of guilt she felt at being the cause. Her mother, on the other hand, was furious.

'Well, what do you call this?' said Raine. 'We've been out of our minds with worry. We've been everywhere! Even to some strange tower in the middle of the Howling Woods, where we heard that you'd been locked up! The tower refused to let us in until Juniper threatened to blow it up. We finally got in, only to discover that there was no witch to be found, and that you had disappeared . . .' She broke off when she saw, behind Willow, *Moreg Vaine*.

She swallowed. 'Um, Moreg, hello.'

'Good day?' said Moreg, observing them with eyes like razors.

'I – well, we were just explaining to Willow that we were concerned about her. She appeared to have run off – but I see you must have found her!'

'Actually, Raine, she found me.'

Raine's eyes popped. 'Is that true?'

'Yes,' Moreg said, glancing from her to Willow's sisters with a meaningful look.

'Oh.'

Willow looked at her mother and said, 'Mum, I know you were just trying to help, but you'd help me a lot more if you would just listen to me.'

'I do listen, Willow, of course I do. You were unwell,

your magic was . . . behaving rather oddly. We needed to get you help, my dear.'

Moreg raised an eyebrow, looking from Raine to Willow's father, Hawthorn. 'I do not wish to get involved in family matters, but I can say this: in future, when your daughter asks for me, please send a raven at once.'

Willow grinned as Raine blinked at Moreg in shock.

Moreg turned to leave, then she stopped and looked back at Juniper and Camille. 'Oh yes, before I forget. For the record, Willow is not ill, mad or a liar. Tuesday did get lost, and we did, in fact, go and find it.'

'*What?*' said Camille as the witch left.

Willow followed Moreg outside to see her go, and her family trailed in her wake. They watched Moreg's tall form as she strode up the garden path, then got on to her impressive broom. Its twin engines roared to life, spitting flames as she flew up and away.

Willow looked up at her parents and was shocked when her mother reached forward and hugged her hard. 'I was so worried about you,' she said. Then she let her go and met her eyes. 'I'll listen more, and try to believe you even if it sounds impossible, all right?'

Willow bit her lip, and then hugged her tight, reaching a hand towards her father who squeezed hers in return.

Juniper and Camille watched Moreg's broom as it disappeared beyond the horizon.

Camille muttered, 'You know, they say she's a bit bonkers herself. Can we really trust what she says? I mean, I heard she lives in the Mists of Mitlaire and has tea parties with the dead . . .'

Willow sighed.

From within the hairy carpetbag there was a faint harrumphing sound. **'Wot a cumberworld.'**

An (Abridged) Oswin to English Dictionary

CARBUNCLE: a pimple or unsightly growth. Used as an insult, as in 'Yew 'orrid carbuncle.'

CUMBERWORLD: someone who is so useless, they just serve to take up space. (Oswin, for the most part, applies this to every member of the Moss family, apart from Willow and the late 'Flossy Mistress'.)

EEL: hell, as in 'what fresh eel is this?'

GIZARD: a very old wizard.

HARPY-HAG: a nagging or highly interfering person.

INFERMEROL: infernal. Many kobolds often hear things incorrectly while hiding in places like beds, or suitcases, or stoves due to their aversion to sunlight and crowds and other scary things, like baths.

LIB-BRAIN: librarian. See *infermerol* for reasons for likely mispronunciation.

PROBERBELLY: probably. See *infermerol* for reasons for likely mispronunciation.

SQUIFFLESTICKS: something that has gone more than a bit wrong.

SLEW: slur (an insinuation that is seen to damage someone's reputation or character).

Acknowledgements:

One of the best parts of being an author is being lucky enough to work with such incredibly talented people, and I think when it comes to children's publishing this is even more true. To my wonderful editor, Harriet Wilson, who brings so much joy, warmth and magic in all that she does, I feel incredibly lucky to work with you. You have made this an enormous joy from the start. Thank you so much for your belief and support for Starfell – it has meant the world.

I am fortunate enough to have another editor too, in the wondrous form of Julia Sanderson. She not only takes the time and trouble to help me fix every long, winding sentence I waffle on with (I'm sorry!) with her deft hands, always with such warmth and kindness (which is the truly remarkable part – her incredible grace in the face of such wanton comma abuse), but has also helped me untangle more plot threads than Oswin could hide in a carpetbag from. Thank you so much, lovely!

Enormous praise and thanks to Sarah Warburton, kindred spirit and artist extraordinaire, for bringing Starfell to life. Each one of your incredible illustrations – from the small, detailed ones to the epic spreads – are gasp-worthy and have made me pinch myself on more occasions than I can count.

I'm not sure how I got lucky enough to have you work on Starfell, but I can only thank all the stars above.

To Helen Boyle, my wonderful, guardian-angel agent, I couldn't have navigated this world without you. Thank you for being there for me, encouraging and supporting me (making me my own hairy green carpetbag!) and most of all just being one of my most favourite people, ever.

To Sean Williams, thank you so much for another amazing cover – you blew me away! You are next-level talented and I'm so grateful for all that you've done in shaping the series.

Elorine Grant, thank you so much for the beautiful, immersive text design. You are a marvel. Thank you so much for bringing the words to life! Also, thank you for inspiring the weather dial in Library. You might recall that last year at a team lunch you mentioned that if you ever had a library of your own, you'd like it to always be winter inside so that you could have a roaring fire year-round – well, that bit was for you!

To everyone at HarperCollins – thank you for making dreams come true, and for all the fun, warmth and joy you bring. A special thank you to: Ann-Janine Murtagh, Jo-Anna Parkinson, Geraldine Stroud, Val Braithwaite, David McDougall, Ryan Hammond, Margot Lohan, Katie Ashworth, Pippa Poole, Louisa Sheridan, Jessica Dean, Alex Cowan,

Beth Maher, Rebecca Fortuin, Tanya Hougham, Harriet Williams, Deborah Wilton and Nicole Linhardt-Rich.

To my wonderful, supportive husband, Rui, thank you for everything you do – from helping to inspire Oswin with your silliness to trying to help me win the unwinnable fight to meet my deadlines, and for always, always providing a supportive shoulder. I couldn't do this without you.

Thank you so much to my wonderful friends and family for all their love and support – Mom, Dad, Simon, Dylan and the best in-laws, Joao and Didi Valente. To my BFF, Catherine Zamojski – thank you for all your kindness and support for my writing over the years. And to my lovely Suffolk bunch, Suzie, Neil, Bob and Helen, you are the best.

It is truly wonderful when anyone likes what you have written but to receive praise from writing legends Robin Stevens, Michelle Harrison, P. G. Bell, Laura Ellen Anderson and Stephanie Burgis had me beaming like a lunatic. Thank you!

To all the readers, booksellers, teachers, librarians and bloggers who have shared their enthusiasm and support for Starfell – thank you so much. I truly hope you enjoy Willow's next adventure!

Read on for a glimpse of the next book in the Starfell series . . .

STARFELL

Willow Moss and the Vanished Kingdom

Dear Sir,

We are proud to be sending our youngest child, Willow Moss, to attend your school. What a time to be alive! We — her parents — are delighted at the amendment to the treaty, allowing for the integrated education of magical and non-magical children under the age of thirteen for the first time in Starfell's history. I can only imagine your own excitement — I wish I was there to witness it!

I can't foresee a teacher of your fine calibre having any doubts about managing someone with a magical ability. (No doubt there has been rigorous training for the new endeavour, and I trust that only the most stalwart of educators have made the grade.) However, if you experience even a slight, momentary twinge of concern, have no fear! I can reassure you that in sending you Willow, who is the least dangerous of my three witch daughters, there will be little danger of her blowing up one of your students or sending them hurtling through the sky with her mind! (Kids, am I right?)

Though, admittedly, there is the small but, alas, real danger that she might make one or all of the children disappear due to a new ability she acquired in recent months. (We blame puberty, it's havoc.) Nonetheless, rest assured in the knowledge that, for the most part, she has this under control — apart from when she sneezes — and is able to return those she has vanished fairly unscathed. No doubt this will offer complete comfort all round.

In terms of her educational background, Willow has been home-schooled by her granny — the renowned potion-maker Florence Moss — who has sadly passed on. However, as my mother-in-law had lost most of her marbles while she was still alive, due to a potion explosion in the mountains of Nach, this probably means you have your work cut out for you. Sorry.

Sincerely,

Raine Moss
Resident witch of neighbouring Grinfog, renowned seer and creator of the Travelling Fortune Fair*

*Tickets available by raven, half-price entry to the Midnight Market (sale offer for the period of the Greening Moon)

Discover where Willow's
story begins . . .

The magic is waiting...

STARFELL

Willow Moss and
the Lost Day

DOMINIQUE VALENTE

Illustrated by SARAH WARBURTON